Hot Lesbian Romance Collection

Just Bae

Copyright © 2022 by Just Bae

All rights reserved.

No part of this book may be reproduced in any form or by any electronic or mechanical means, including information storage and retrieval systems, without written permission from the author, except for the use of brief quotations in a book review.

Contents

Celeste

Chapter 1	3
Chapter 2	5
Chapter 3	8
Chapter 4	13
Chapter 5	20
Chapter 6	23
Chapter 7	28
Chapter 8	33
Chapter 9	41

Taylor

Chapter 1	47
Chapter 2	50
Chapter 3	52
Chapter 4	54
Chapter 5	59
Chapter 6	64
Chapter 7	73

Rebecca

Chapter 1	79
Chapter 2	85
Chapter 3	88
Chapter 4	92

Chapter 5	100
Chapter 6	105

Amber

Prologue	109
Chapter 1	113
Chapter 2	118
Chapter 3	123
Chapter 4	135
Chapter 5	141

Celeste

Chapter One

My girlfriend and I were fooling around on Sandy Island, Anguilla for a bit when we saw a young black woman paddling towards the private area in an old canoe. She was lithe but curvaceous, dressed in a lime green bikini with black strings, clearly designed to emphasize her cleavage. Her figure would have needed an acre of fabric to cover those great-looking breasts and ass cheeks.

The woman's body was magical; every movement of hers was timed and cordial. As she'd leant over, her bikini struggled to contain her assets. The cords of her G-string barely covered her hole.

Celeste, my girlfriend, caught me staring. "Wipe that drool from your chin, sweetie."

"Sorry, I was looking so hard, wasn't I?"

"Yup," Celeste sat up and gazed with me. "Damn, though."

"I know, right!"

We watched her drag her canoe onto the sand, all the way to the other side of the bay. We looked on as the woman used a flick-knife from the boat to make some thin shavings, then effortlessly lit them. Within an hour, she put together a kindling and made a campfire. When she was finished, she bent over to push the canoe back into the water, giving us a perfect view of her sexy romp.

* * *

"You were thinking about fucking her, weren't you?" Celeste asked. *It was pointless to deny it; the girl resembled a girl on the beach in a Sports Illustrated magazine bikini edition.* I looked at Celeste, my eyebrow raised. I knew her, very well, and she admitted what I already knew. "Yeah, okay. I was thinking about fucking her too. God, what an ass!"

"Really? I didn't look down that far," I said. Celeste swatted at me.

"I can be your little canoe girl if you like," Celeste said pulling me down on top of her.

Chapter Two

The day I met Celeste must have been the luckiest in my life. A meeting at a social gathering and I'd found my soulmate; *someone who got me, who was interested in me for me and not for my money.* Celeste was as dirty and playful as they come. It was a welcomed change from the stuck-up bitches that Tinder had sent my way. We also had similar tastes in women. She'd point out hotties to me, and we'd share texts about them and what we would do to them. There were also encounters where one of both of us seduced another woman into our bed for an evening or two.

How we got here...

Now, we're here for a week to celebrate our engagement, to an exclusive resort on the Caribbean island of Anguilla. It was so remote that we'd had to take a jet, then a prop-seaplane and finally a boat to get there. The good thing about Anguilla was the need for its island guests' privacy. The suites were far enough apart that even Celeste's wild screaming wouldn't be heard miles away.

* * *

That first night, we didn't even make it out of our room. It had been a long day of traveling, trapped in other people's company, and we'd had our hands off each other for too long. Suitcases dumped just inside the door, we ignored everything else, found the bedroom, and went for each other.

Celeste tapped my head, and I came up for air.

"I think room service is at the door," she said. "You'll have to go, I'm a little tied up at the moment." I'm sure she could have pulled free of the scarves if she wanted, but that would have spoiled our little game.

"Sorry, I couldn't hear anything with your thighs against my ears," I said. I rose, wrapped a nearby robe around myself, and went to open the door. An island girl, pretty and busty, pushed the trolley through into the living room. My eyes were drawn to her chest - her uniform's blouse was straining at the buttons, and I could peek through the gap to the bounty inside. Her nametag read Alesha.

"You sign?" The young woman presented me with the tab, and I signed it. As I passed it back to her, I noticed she'd been looking towards the bedroom, where Celeste was on full display.

"Enjoy your evening, ladies," Alesha said with a wink. I watched her fine ass sway out of the door, then took the plates straight through to the bedroom.

"Strawberries and whip cream, how terribly English of you," Celeste remarked.

"I'd turn a few heads eating them like this at Wimbledon," I said, spooning some cream onto her breasts, before eating it back off. The coolness of the cream made Celeste's nipples poke up, all the more sensitive for my lips and tongue to tease.

The strawberries I spread underneath her and sprayed her cunt with whip cream.

"I hear strawberries make your cum taste sweeter, baby," I said.

"I'm all yours," Celeste said reclining back.

Chapter Three

Celeste was very much a morning-sex person, and she dragged me off the path into a dense tree region round the edge of the resort. I held her legs while she leant back against a tree, and we brought each other in the privacy of nature, with the sound of wildlife chirping all around us. We'd pushed on through the tree area, to find another secluded beach beyond, completely deserted. I put our cooler down, and we laid back against it, looking out at the crystal-clear pale blue water.

It wasn't long before Celeste had removed her clothes and laid on the towel, sunning herself. I drizzled sunscreen lotion across her back, and knelt astride her waist and massaged her shoulders before sliding my hands further down. I teased the side of her small breasts as I worked down towards her hips. Then I turned, working her legs, caressing her feet and sliding my fingers between her toes.

"Oh, baby that feels so good..." Celeste moaned as I worked back up her legs, onto her thighs. She parted and I slid my hands up further to caress her derriere. As I worked her glutes, Celeste pulled her knees wide and raised off the towel. My fingers were now inside her; she was wet and waiting.

"God, what you do to me," she said. I shuffled forward on my knees and slowly dipped down, my hands were resting on her hips. *Long sucking clicking sounds echoing nature; we had all day, literally. What could be more perfect than making love to my beautiful woman this paradise of an island?*

With Celeste's favorite dildo, I toyed with my girl's clit, dipping in, and out. It wasn't long before she came, cursing and praising. After Celeste caught her breath, she rolled over onto her back.

"I'm on top now," she said.

"No way, I'm not getting sand in my hair today," I said.

"What did I say?" Celeste said as she climbed on top of me before I had a chance to counter. "Now what?"

It was a great view as my girl's pretty hairless cunt lowered into my mouth. She grabbed the dildo and started fucking me with it, both of us moaned amid the morning waves.

* * *

The only other person we saw all morning was a black girl who from a distance resembled the one we were ogling yesterday. The woman paddled towards our area right when Celeste and I finished making out. Then, she pulled her canoe up onto land, and headed over to the area the other woman had gone yesterday. She rekindled the fire and took a frame from the canoe and erected it over the embers. After that, she placed a pan on top. We watched her amazed at how she carried the fish in big baskets on top of her head. Then, she laid them the fish out on the beach, gutted them out, and then put them on a makeshift grill. When she filled the grill with enough fish, she turned to us, and beckoned us over.

"Now that's the life," Celeste said. "Catching your own food, cooking it in the open. Sexy and resourceful, what's not to like about this one?"

"You've got it bad, don't you?" I joked reaching into our cooler for a few beers to take over.

* * *

"Sorry to disturb you over there with the smoke," the woman said as she fanned the flames.

"No, not at all. It smells delicious. Did you catch the fish yourself?" Celeste said.

"Yes, I did. There are plenty of different kinds in this area," the woman said continued fanning the flames.

"I bet," I replied.

"Come and sit. You are our guests," the woman gestured.

Celeste and I sat and held hands while the woman grilled fish.

* * *

We ate surprisingly with our fingers and on silver foil. She continued cooking and noticed that we were looking at the stockpiles of fish in her canoe. "For my family," she said. "Must cook fresh, or they'll go bad."

* * *

The woman told us her story - of how she got the job working at the resort. The wages were low and her mother also worked as a cleaner there as well. When she introduced herself as Alesha, we realized she was the girl who came to our room yesterday and saw Celeste spread on the bed. "I'm so sorry, I have such a poor memory for faces. And you were wearing a lot more, the last time I saw you," Celeste said.

"Yes. That shitty uniform, I hate it. But you're wearing much more than when I last saw you!"

Celeste was not one who was easily embarrassed, but that made her blush. Alesha was a little nervous when Celeste didn't respond to her last comment.

"No, please. Sex is normal, healthy and a big part of life. Love freely and enjoy being young!" Alesha said making Celeste and I laugh.

* * *

We chatted on the beach for the best part of the afternoon, finishing off the beers and snacks I brought from the minibar. Celeste put on her favorite Spotify playlist, and we started dancing. But all too soon, Alesha had to leave. "I must go, and take the fish to my family. I hope to see you again!"

"You know where to find us," Celeste said, watching Alesha's nice ass sashay back to the canoe. "Damn, that girl is so fine."

"I do agree," I said, shaking my head thinking about how her breasts all but escaped from her bikini. "She sure is."

Chapter Four

That evening, we were just wondering which restaurant to try out, when we heard a knocking at the patio doors. It was Alesha, in a loose flowing brown-patterned dress, hair pinned up, carrying a basket.

"Good evening," I said, opening the door. Alesha smiled, as she stepped inside. She reached into the basket and pulled out a bottle.

"You like rum?"

"Hell yeah!" Celeste said.

Alesha laid out three shot glasses on the counter and had poured out a measure into each. "This is good. It's made here."

Celeste picked hers up and sniffed at it. *What an ass?*

I went to take a sip and "No," Alesha said. "We drink together, all of it."

I held my glass and waited. "3, 2, 1, Go!" and we chugged the shots down. I coughed and Celeste and Alesha laughed at me.

We had another shot, and another - *this doesn't taste so bad after all.*

* * *

Our conversation went on for hours like we were old friends. I realized Alesha was flirting with me. Or rather, us - she kept touching Celeste's arm as she was my hand, and I caught them checking each other out. This, I thought, was going to get interesting.

I didn't have to wait long.

"I hate air conditioning. I'm going outside to the jacuzzi. Wanna join me?" Alesha stood, and headed for the door.

* * *

Night had fallen, and the lighting made the patio are look qquite exotic. As she walked through the suite, Alesha pushed the straps of her dress off her shoulders, and let the material slide down her body and drop to the floor. Celeste and I watched, mouths agape, as she walked naked through the patio doors and onto the veranda.

Alesha looked back over her shoulder, "Will you join me?"

"Yes, ma'am," Celeste said. "I sure will!" With that, she pulled her top over her head, unclipped her bra along the way and tossing it aside. I followed them, struggling out of my shorts and snatching up the bottle of rum, just in time to watch my girl and Alesha stepping down into the jacuzzi.

They were giggling, feeling naughty. I walked over the decking towards them. The good view of two pairs of tits jostling and shimmering in the bubble jets was turning me on. I stepped down into the water and took a seat opposite of Celeste and Alesha, who were sat side by side.

"Well, isn't this nice," I said, taking a swig and passing it around.

Celeste, being the femme she was, started the fireworks early.

"Being naked isn't taboo here, huh?" Celeste asked.

"No, Sex is a normal and healthy part of life." Alesha continued on this topic for a while; as she was talking, I felt a foot stroking up my calf. I glanced over at Celeste, but she was giving nothing away, focused on Alesha.

"All love is good. If people make each other happy, how can anyone complain?"

Celeste's foot worked its way up my leg, and soon

enough was in my lap, rubbing my inner thighs. I looked down, and saw that Alesha's foot had joined hers.

"You ladies, what are you up to?" I said.

Celeste gave me a look "Nothing, just getting comfortable."

Alesha and Celeste had changed positions, leaning towards each other slightly. They began stroking each other.

Celeste gave me another look - a desperate pleading one. I knew what that meant.

"Well, would you look at that, we're all out of rum," I said, waving the empty bottle. "Let me just pop inside and grab another."

* * *

Celeste preferred to work alone to get things started. I stood, wrapped a towel around me and went inside.

While pottering around indoors, I glanced back out to the veranda. Celeste was kneeling on the seat of the jacuzzi, leaning over Alesha, and they were kissing so deeply. Alesha legs were spread, allowing Celeste to finger her; in return Alesha was sliding her hand up Celeste's thigh, and slipped her fingers into her while stroking her clit. I looked away, before the girls looked up and saw me.

* * *

I scooped up another bottle from the bar and headed back outside. The soft lighting above warmed the wooden veranda. The underwater lighting cast blue-white ripples around the alcove in which the sunken jacuzzi lay. Celeste was sitting on the side of the spa, leaning back, head tossed back and eyes closed. As I got closer, I saw Alesha laying across the water, ass cheeks bobbing out of the jets, with her head planted between Celeste's thighs. Hearing those pleasing, whimpering, begging noises coming from my girl made my pussy so wet. I stood in the doorway for a moment, enjoying the scene of vanilla and chocolate. Nothing gave me more enjoyment than watching Celeste being taken over.

"Oh fuck, you're good," Celeste panted.

"You like it, huh?" Alesha said.

"Hell yeah! Girl, your tongue is—" Celeste moaned.

When I came out, Celeste looked over at me and said. "I need you. Bring that pussy over here. I want to taste it." Experience had shown me the more, Celeste was being worked over, the hornier she got, and the better head she gave. I lower onto her face; my cunt vanished between her lips and face. She was gagging, eating me out like she was starving,

I reached down to grasp one of her breasts and Alesha sucked the other while fingering and eating my Celeste out. While I was playing with Celeste's nipple, I could feel her convulsing every few seconds. Alesha was sucking the soul out of my baby.

I might have been the one who moaned the loudest especially when Alesha joined Celeste in eating me out from both sides; Celeste on my pussy and Alesha in my ass.

We were moaning in unison and Celeste whispered to Alesha, *"You're next."*

"Anything you want, girl?" She responded as they continued working me over. Their breasts were swinging back and forth in the bubbles and I was getting close to coming.

* * *

A combination of naughty talk, rum, and sight of two of the most exotic women in front of me was becoming too much to bear. Celeste and Alesha's moans got me so horny. They pushed their heads harder into my pussy and ass, in perfect rhythm, licking and sucking away. My pussy was throbbing uncontrollably until seconds later, my Celeste's throat opened.

"Here she comes..." Celeste yelled.

"Oh shit, baby! Right there, right there, I'm going to come..." I panted.

Celeste and Alesha quickly got up just in time.

I squirted over their faces, chests, and down their laps.

Alesha couldn't even open her eyes. *I never squirted as much as this before.*

"Look what your girl has done. I can't even open my eyes," Alesha said, leaning over landing on Celeste's face. Celeste rubbed it and started licking some of it off.

"My girl must really like you..."

We giggled.

"This was supposed to be my day off," Alesha said as Celeste rubbed her. Alesha, in the meantime, started rubbing my pussy again. She then leaned forward, and I reached over, and we were kissing. I tasted my juices on her lips; that intoxicating scent that never failed to drive me wild. She fingered me gently and I was on the verge of coming again.

Celeste then took one of Alesha's fingers from my cunt and put them up to her mouth. They both sucked it and it was a sight to see.

"Let's take this inside," I said, "It's getting cold out here."

Chapter Five

Alesha laid back on our king-size bed, head propped on a pillow, ass on the edge, with her legs over Celeste's shoulders. Celeste kneeled on the floor and licked away. *Alesha was my Celeste's prey to devour.*

I laid back in my chair in the corner, beer in hand and enjoyed the show. Alesha was peering through the valley of her cleavage, she moaned as Celeste teased and coaxed her toward climaxing. Celeste then grabbed one of Alesha's black jugs in her small hand and entered her large nipple into her mouth. "Suck it, baby!" Alesha panted, cradling Celeste's face as she suckled. Celeste, in the meantime, slid her fist inside Alesha's big wet cunt and hit her G-spot.

"Fuck!" Alesha shouted.

I honestly felt bad for Alesha but the smacks of

Celeste's fist going in and out and soft moans of both gave me little concern.

Celeste pulled out her wet hand, brought her coated fingers to Alesha's other breast, and painted Alesha's cum over her areola and nipple. After that, she leaned across to lick and suck it back off. Alesha reached for Celeste's hand and brought it to her lips, one by one licking and sucking herself off. They stared at each other, kissing slowly and deeply.

Breaking the kiss, they both knew what the other was thinking. Celeste put her leg over Alesha's chest, lowered her pussy over her mouth, then went back down to resume eating her out. Tits pressed against abs, legs wrapped round faces, I watched them; a perfect mix-n-match.

* * *

My pussy was so wet. I stood, and walked slowly over to the bed. I sat back and started fingering myself.

"Let me help you with that," Celeste said replacing her tongue in Alesha' clit with her fingers. I watched, transfixed, as she worked up a circular rhythm over her clit, which she was matching with her tongue on mine. Alesha's pussy looked so inviting, so wet. I knew she was waiting to be fucked.

"Both of you, eat my pussy," Alesha said. I looked at

Celeste, who slipped her lips from my clit and forced me down into her lover. Alesha's vulva was big enough for both of us to eat and be satisfied.

* * *

"She's loving it," Celeste said as we saw Alesha's Adam's Apple moving back and forth. I was working on her clit as Celeste's tongue thrust deep inside. Celeste was grabbing her boobs and Alesha was squeezing her nipples. My gaze fell on Alesha's, watching her tits jump and bounce each time I hit her G-spot.

"Yeah babe, lick that pussy..." Celeste urged me. Alesha's orgasm was on its way. I moaned to speed up the action seeing Alesha's chest heaving and her abs twitching. Moments later, she was coming. "Fuck, oh yeah! I—" Alesha yelled rocking side to side.

Her cum leaked from her pussy, white and creamy in contrast to her dark ebony skin. Celeste looked at me and I knew what she was thinking, We went down, ate Alesha's cum together; swapping as it kept coming out.

Chapter Six

I lay in the middle of the bed, exhausted. Each woman beside me, with one leg cocked over mine and their tits pressed into my chest. Alesha's head was on my shoulder and Celeste nuzzling at my neck. Celeste and I had a lot of sex this weekend and it was seriously starting to take its toll on me.

"What are we now going to do with you," Celeste panted, her tongue in my ear and fingers rubbing my chest.

"Yes, we must have you again," Alesha said, leaning forward to lick my nipple, her hand reached down to cup my crotch. Her touch felt amazing, but I needed Celeste to bring me to ecstasy.

"Help me," Alesha said to Celeste, moving her head down my body. They kissed their way down my chest, over my abs towards my groin. They spread my legs and then started kissing inside my thighs. Alesha sucked on me from the front and Celeste from the back.

"Sheesh, you girls are so fucking good!" I panted. "Fuck!" I screamed when both tongues hit my G-spots at once. *No-one had ever done that for me before.*

Alesha giggled, then kept licking my ass while my pussy was sucked by Celeste. Then Celeste put her middle finger in me and pushed it against my walls.

"Oh, my fucking god," I screamed again. Alesha worked her finger slowly back and forth in my ass as Celeste kept sucking on my clit.

* * *

Both women mastered making me climax multiple times. I knew Celeste wanted Alesha again but so did I.

"Get on top of her," Celeste said. "I want you to come on my girl's fucking face, Alesha. I'll let you two fuck your brains out while I take a break."

Alesha smiled and crawled on top of me. Celeste guided her vagina into my face before retiring to the chair to watch.

Alesha was good but not as good as my Celeste. She squirmed and bounced too much which was irking at times. I tried grabbing onto one of her big tits as she was facefucking me. My small hands barely held onto it; each was almost as big as my head. As Alesha bounced on my face, I wiggled my way back up for air. She looked disappointed but then I said, "Give me your milk, baby, I want those milky titties to blast all over me." Alesha raised her eyebrows as I started kissing my way into the depths of her cleavage, burying my face between her tits, tasting her sweat. I was in heaven, hearing Alesha's gasps for me to stop; she let out odd curses which made me even more determined. After nearly suckling her for a few minutes, those big breasts started to milk; streams ran down her ebony skin and they were starting to wet our bedsheets.

"You did it, baby!" Celeste hollered from across the room.

I must have open the valve because Alesha's cunt begin squirting in all directions just after a few touches. I didn't let up until she finished spraying nearly reaching Celeste.

"Oh fuck," Alesha panted. "How did you make me come like that, girl?"

"I learned this from Celeste over there," I laughed, as Alesha pushed me back down onto my back.

***

Alesha towered over me, her breasts swayed and danced. "Let me help you with her. I know her better than anyone," Celeste said as she stepped over to the bed, climbed on board, and knelt across my chest facing

Alesha. She leaned forward to kiss her. I enjoyed watching a bit of girl-on-girl, but I couldn't see much from this angle; Celeste took away my view of Alesha's juicy tits. Then, she lowered herself onto my face.

* * *

I slid my tongue into her cunt and enjoyed her. Celeste Alesha were moaning loudly; the wet sounds of their kisses and pussies being working on each end of me. It was galling that I couldn't see how we all looked in the room's mirror, but my mind painted the perfect picture.

I was about to release and I got lightheaded. Then, finally I did; the word I screamed into Celeste's warm depths, *fuccccccckkkkkkk!* That's all I remembered...

* * *

I wasn't out for long - *I don't think* - just long enough for Celeste to know that I reached my limit for the night.

"I should go," Alesha said, picking up her dress and throwing it back on. "I'll lose my job if they find me here."

"We wouldn't feel right, letting you leave in the middle of the night. Stay here, get some rest, and leave when there's sunlight," Celeste said. She patted the bed beside me.

"Okay but—" Alesha said.

"Don't worry. We're all out of gas for tonight..." Celeste patted Alesha on her back.

* * *

We snuggled and I spooned in behind Celeste, who draped herself over Alesha. It wasn't long before I dozed off, one of my arms draped across Celeste but the other on Alesha's huge breast. Celeste might have made out with Alesha again, but I was too zoned out to care.

* * *

The sunlight was streaming through the windows, and I woke up to my usual morning routine of poking Celeste in the butt. I looked up and saw Alesha had made off. I guessed she took off at dawn, like Celeste suggested.

I put my arm round her waist, kissed her on her shoulder. "I love you so much," I said.

She rolled over, "I love you too. Wow, what a night!"

"Yeah. I'm a bit sore after all that—"

"S-E-X," we said at the same time.

"Give me some before we get up," Celeste said, pushing my head into her lap. She spread her legs and welcomed me into a new day.

Chapter Seven

For our last night at the resort, we got dressed up for a night at the local casino. Celeste had on a lacy sheer outfit that covered what was legally required but little else. Her skirt had a leg slit so high she needn't have bothered wearing it at all. I donned my blazer, bowtie, and slouchy pants. Then, we hit the tables.

Lady Luck smiled on us that evening; we lost a little at first and then made back more than double. I enjoyed seeing men watching my Celeste as she danced and jumped, bouncing her assets perhaps to distract them. Maybe she was doing it on purpose as part of her strategy to win.

Afterward, we staggered back to the hotel room, drunk.

"Shit, there's someone outside!" Celeste yelped. Adrenaline kicked in, as I glanced across to the veranda. I saw movement, two figures in our hot tub; one sitting facing away, the other towards us, bobbing up and down...

"Bloody hell, it's Alesha, fucking some guy in our hot tub!" I said.

"What a nerve?" Celeste said. "Move aside and let me watch!"

Two minutes later, Alesha spotted us looking and waved. She then stood up; rivulets of water ran down her sexy body, through her valleys and round her curves. She reached down to grab the guy's dick which appeared to stretch as she pulled him by it. They exited the tub.

"My God, fuck me!" Celeste said.

That guy must have been well over six foot tall and close to that wide in the shoulders, and ripped. The size of his cock was as long as a foot. He was seriously hung; I'd never seen anything like it outside of porn. I was not in the habit of checking out other guy's packages, you understand.

"Yeah, Cobra's about a foot long, so..." I was smiling as I said that but I felt a bit jealous. Celeste and I tried a guy before and that freak was so dominant that we had to call the police on him to get him to leave.

"Jesus, just look at that cock," Celeste said as she turned to face me. "Baby, I love you more than anything."

I was ahead of her. "I bet you'd take that cock home with you if I wasn't around."

Celeste was in a trance watching Cobra walk towards the patio door. "No, baby. You know I wouldn't..."

"I know you so well, Celeste. You're horny, so let's have some fun. It's our last night here."

* * *

Alesha and Cobra aka Ajay came through the door. "I hope you don't mind," she said. "I brought you a gift, to say goodbye." Celeste was already walking over, drawn inexorably to the black Adonis. She stroked her hand across his pecs and ran it down over his abs.

"You like?" Alesha said.

"Oh yes, very much."

Alesha looked back at me. "This is Ajay, he's my best friend."

"I'm sure he is," I said. I leaned against the counter and grabbed a beer from the fridge. Alesha was now kneeling in front of Ajay, looking at Celeste while caressing his thick cock. Celeste knelt too, and they both started to kiss and lick along the length of him. They'd alternated rising to the head, sucking around it, and licking along the shaft down to the balls.

Then Alesha took it, and directed it between Celeste's lips, stroking him into my girl's mouth. He was barely halfway in before I could hear her gag, trying to fit that big monster into her throat. Alesha laughed. "It was many months before I could suck him all. In order for me to do so, I have to lie on my back with my head over the end of the bed."

"I'd like to see that," Celeste panted as she gagged. "But I need him to stuff something else of mine, first." She stood, holding the cock against her stomach.

Ajay looked at me, as if for permission.

"Make her scream, she's all yours."

"My pleasure," he said, effortlessly plucked Celeste up off the floor, and carried her into our bedroom. Alesha took my hand, and pulled me in after them.

* * *

Ajay laid Celeste down on the bed, her ass perched on the edge, raised on some pillows. He was in front of her, smacking with her pussy with his long cock. Given the size of Ajay, I saw the look on Celeste's face; excited but with an edge of trepidation. "Make her come first," I said.

Ajay looked over at Alesha. "Get her ready, baby." Alesha fell to her knees and buried her face between Celeste's thighs almost before Ajay had finished speaking. He knelt behind her, took his monster and put it into Alesha's pussy, fucking her as she ate Celeste out.

Celeste loves oral, and she'd happily lay there having orgasm after orgasm. I'm pretty sure Alesha would just keep eating her all night, too. The problem with Celeste is she'll become tight if she kept coming.

"This isn't gonna work guys," I said. "She'll just keep cumming but she ain't gonna loosen up like that."

"You really know how to turn a girl off, that felt so good," Celeste gasped. "She's right, though. Put that long cock in me."

"Undress her lady," Ajay told Alesha. She swayed over to me, and started unbuttoning my blazer. "Try not to make her come fast," he said. "Tonight, I desire her."

Chapter Eight

I laid next to Celeste on the bed, kissed her, and started making out with her while Alesha was eating me out. "You want Ajay bad, don't you," I panted.

"Oh god yeah!" Celeste thighs and arse were sweating profusely.

"That's my girl, ready to lose her shit over a monster cock. You want me to hear you scream, don't you?" I continued urging my girl on while I was being licked.

"God, yes. So hot knowing you're right here with me," Celeste moaned.

Ajay came over with his cock saluting us. It was so long that all of our hands could have gripped it.

"Yeah, that cobra will be buried inside you very soon. Do you think you can take it?"

"Yes, fuck yes, before I die!"

"Come for me, then, and he's all yours," Alesha said

switching to eat Celeste out. I grabbed her hips and drove her face into her pussy, making the bed shake. Ajay slapped her in the face with his cock. She tried to chase it with her mouth, but Ajay kept whipping it away then slapping on the other side. I grabbed it, opened Celeste's jaw wide and wrapped her lips round the head. Ajay grabbed Celeste's head and started thrusting in her mouth. Celeste's face went red; she gasped while strings of saliva and precum hung between her lips and his cock.

"I think she's ready now," Alesha said switching back to my cunt.

"Please fuck me, fuck me, oh god..." Celeste pulled her knees up and back as Ajay's cock approached. He pushed the head against her soaking lips and gave the smallest of thrusts; it popped in and Celeste's lips sealed round the shaft. My girl's mouth went to an O and her eyes closed. "Oh my god, it's so fucking huge."

"You wanted it..." I panted, Alesha and I were now 69-ing.

"Hell, this thing is killing me," she begged as Ajay was stroking deeper and deeper.

He chuckled when I said, "Don't kill my baby, please."

* * *

As I was making out with Alesha, I poked my head up to see Celeste playing with her clit while Ajay's cock was destroying my girl. Her pussy lips and walls being yanked back each time he withdrew then slammed back in.

A few minutes into the fucking, I found Ajay's pounding far too distracting and more than a little intimidating.

"There's some lube in the drawer," I said, easing Alesha off me and standing up. "I think we'll give you two a bit of privacy." Alesha and I retired to the sofa in the living area while Ajay continued to fuck my girl's brains out ignoring my call to get the lube.

* * *

"You seem upset," Alesha noted. "Jealous maybe?"

"Of course, a bit," I said. "I love her, and I'd do anything for her. This is something she wanted, and it's rare for us to meet anyone - let's just say with Ajay's talents." I sat on the sofa, and Alesha stood in front of me. I reached out for her breasts, stroked them, and leaned back as she sat on my lap... "And she does the same for me," I said, filling my mouth with a mere fraction of Alesha's tit, suckling as much for comfort as from lust.

"You're lucky to have found each other," she said, rocking on me and grinding.

"Yes," I said. Celeste's filthy mouth was running away with her in the bedroom; I gathered progress was being made. Then I heard that familiar escalating scream and knew she was cumming again. I reached round and grabbed Alesha's firm ass as she raised up and lowered her pussy on my face.

"Mmm," Alesha moaned. "Your tongue feels so good inside me." She tossed her hair back, thrusting her pussy lips back and forward onto my lips. Alesha was near coming as I tasted the difference in wetness from her sweet warm wet core. Her deep cleavage hung over the loveseat as she rode my face slowly. Meanwhile, I was listening to Celeste getting fucked badly in the other room.

"Finger my ass," Alesha ordered. I reached round behind her, sliding down a little so I could reach it. She raised her head and gasped. I started working her pussy and ass in and out, feeling myself getting wetter by the moment.

"You's a bad girl," Alesha said, driving herself harder onto me as she got closer to coming. I started rocking her ass up and down, making her moan and groan.

"Yes, now, yes," she panted, and I felt her flooding, and her arse and pussy pulsing.

"Come for me, come for mommy..."

Alesha yelled, "Fuuuuuckkkkk!" Her voice echoed the suite and nearly causing a glass on the table to fall.

**

"I want to watch them again," Alesha said, climbing off

me and heading back to the bedroom. Celeste wasn't hardly making any noises, so I was curious, too.

She was kneeling on the bed, clinging to the headboard for dear life while Ajay took her from behind. "God, yes, oh shit, fuck me, just keep fucking me," Celeste panted. Her voice was hoarse from the screaming earlier and there was a huge wet patch on the bed underneath them. Ajay was grunting, his big balls swinging as he thrust into her. Both were sweating bullets; many were running down his back, and Celeste looked like a 70-s rock star with panda-eyeliner running down her cheeks.

"That's my girl," I said, and gave her a kiss on the lips. She was panting and gasping between involuntary swears. Her arms gave way and she braced her head and chest on the pillows. Alesha was now kneeling beside Ajay, and they were kissing. Then she moved behind him, laid down, and slid her head back between his legs, then started licking his ass and Celeste's pussy and clit while Ajay continued to drive into her. She reached up and grabbed Celeste's hips, pulling her down and forcing the pace of her rocking back onto Ajay's monster cock.

"Oh my god—oh my god," Celeste yelled, trying to look round at what the pair were doing to her. I had a great view of Alesha's pussy; red, swollen and creamy. I knelt before her and stole a taste, then buried my head between her thighs, licking and eating her cream. I reached under with my hand and slid fingers back into her ass as I ate her out; that made her attack Ajay and Celeste more.

"Get on your back," Ajay said, pulling Celeste away from the headboard. I stood and Alesha rolled out from underneath them, her face smeared with precum. Ajay flipped Celeste over without even pulling out, dropped her to the mattress and started pounding her. *This might have been the endgame.* Celeste pulled her knees up against her tits as Ajay slammed, smacking her clit with his pelvic bone with each thrust. I looked at Celeste's face; tears were rolling down her cheeks, eyes rolled back so far they were nearly white, freaking me out. She was mouthing something, but words had left her.

Finally, Ajay gave way. His balls were pumping hard, and cum boiled from Celeste's pussy as he held himself fully inside her as he came. Then he withdrew, still coming, and shot ropes of his jizz up from Celeste's pussy, across her stomach and tits and up to her face. She laid there, whimpering, drained, but satisfied.

I stood, transfixed, watching my girl's gaping pussy twitch. I could have easily slid my whole hand inside, though I daren't; she must have been so sore, her pussy looked red and angry.

* * *

I looked at Celeste, sated, covered in Ajay's cum. She

had never looked more beautiful. I kissed on her forehead, then put a bottle of water on the bedside cabinet next to her. It sure looked like she'd lost a lot of fluids.

I caught Alesha's eye, and smirked. "Look what your best friend has done," I said, echoing her words from the other day. "You need to clean her up." She climbed onto the bed. Starting at Celeste's neck, she slowly sucked and licked her way down my girl's body, taking special care of her breasts and her navel, until eventually she reached Celeste's pussy.

"Yes... But by god, be gentle," Celeste pleaded.

"Yes, madam," Alesha replied, and she got to work.

Alesha's ass bobbed in front of me as she suckled on Celeste's clit. I couldn't stop staring. "Take care of her, Alesha," Ajay said. I approached the bed, knelt behind her. Alesha felt the bed move and arched her back, dropping her ches and presenting herself to me. I pulled those asscheeks aside, rested my tip against her, and pushed.

She groaned right into Celeste's cunt. "Be gentle, remember," I admonished, sliding my tongue into her tight ass. *I wondered if Ajay ever rode this ass; I guess he must have.* I tried not to look over, but there he was, stroking himself back to hardness.

* * *

It was weird to feel a guy moving inside me, his cock was so big but I have to admit, it felt good. It made Celeste happy, so I did it. Ajay's huge cock pounded my thin walls, and now I was screaming in pleasure. Meanwhile, I was watching Celeste go bug-eyed...as Alesha snatched my girl's soul once again.

Chapter Nine

Dawn broke on our last day on Anguilla. Alesha and Ajay had gone, slipped out in the night after Celeste and I had passed out. My last clear memory was the two of us lying on our backs, side by side and holding hands, kissing and confessing our love for each other, while Ajay buried his cock in my pussy, and Alesha rode me, slapping my face with her huge tits.

"Morning, beautiful," I said.

"Sup?" Celeste mumbled.

"You okay? Seemed rather intense for you last night."

"My cunt's gonna be out-of-order for a week!"

"I reckon. I'll go get us some coffee."

"Can you close that window while you're up, please, it's cracking my head open."

***

I fiddled around our living quarters, looking at the wreckage of our memorable night. We'd cleaned out the minibar and there were empties everywhere. Cum-stained cushions and bits of our clothing were scattered over the floor. But *thank god* there was coffee. I put the coffee maker on, when my eyes fell to the silver dish on the side table; the dish I dropped our casino winnings onto...they were now not there. Maybe Celeste had put them away?

I was worried, looking around everywhere. I couldn't find our money nor my second-best Rolex watch that Celeste got me. Her diamond stud earrings were gone, too.

"The fuck... Those fuckers ripped us off!" I started crashing around the place, looking under stuff I'd already moved. We'd been so stupid to trust Alesha and Ajay in our place. Thank God all our credit cards, passports and stuff were locked away in our room's safe.

***

"Hey, babe, calm down and keep the noise down, will ya?"

"I knew I shouldn't have trusted them."

"What the fuck's going on?" Celeste came into the living room.

"We got robbed."

"Shit!"

"That damn Ajay!"

"At least he's got a big dick," Celeste teased. "Look, does it really matter?"

"You don't feel like we've been taken advantage of?"

"Hmm," she said, playing with my hair. "What memories are worth taking away from this place! Just call it a few hundred dollars tip?"

"But—"

"Quit ya bitching. We've got a half-hour or so before the boat arrives to get us," Celeste said, pulling on the tie of her silk robe which fell open revealing her naked self."

I wrapped my arms round her waist. "Are you never satisfied?" I asked rubbing her clit.

"Nuh," she said, kissing me. "Let's go get ready." Celeste smacked my ass and I hurried forward.

The End

Taylor

Chapter One

The faint patter of rain rattled against the window as Taylor Moore prepared for her last OnlyFans session for the evening. The rain and fog in Atlanta at this time of year was so thick only the pale white glow of lamps in her neighborhood lined the street. Nothing could be seen except a faint neon glow coming from a second-floor window of a townhouse at the far end of the row.

Taylor's space was small yet neat with an open and stereotypical minimalist architecture. She had a plethora of leafy plants, pastel furniture, LED lighting strips, and stacked floral paintings. Chill Hip-Hop was playing in the background making its atmosphere warming and exotic.

Taylor, dressed in a white midriff sweater cut right at the center of her boobs and nothing else below, posed provocatively in front of her computer. Her glam long lashes, glassy pink nails along with her makeup and long wavy hair made her look so much the part of a classic pin up with a modern-day twist.

Her breasts fitted perfectly in her midriff sweater revealing her toned abs. It was a body that Taylor spent hours on the treadmill daily while maintaining a strict diet.

"Well guys this was fun! But it's time for me to go, I'm tired and it's late—" Taylor said to her screen that pings while she talks, Each 'ping' is a small tip from a crop of users, all of them saying *'don't go...'*

"Nice try but I took the vibrator out, you can try again tomorrow! Same time, boys. Think about me at work and I'll be here right after, okay? Don't forget to follow me..."

Taylor signed off for the evening and covered her laptop's camera.

Eyeing her last dab for the evening, Taylor huffed and puffed seeing she was out of CBD oil. She pondered running to Lonnie's Pot Shop about fifteen minutes away to get some more before heading to bed. The rain had slackened up and Taylor believed she could make it in time before they closed at eleven. The time was twelve minutes after ten.

I hope Nikki is there.

Nikki was her favorite budtender at Lonnie's who

usually gave her more for her money than the other workers.

Taylor didn't want Nikki see her the way she was. It would take nearly an hour to remove all the makeup off her and get changed. Taylor grunted, pushing herself up off the floor and snatched off her wig. She rushed into the bathroom and removed her makeup as much as possible.

Taylor looked entirely different from her cam persona; small freckles and her eyebrows are much sparser. Leaning into the mirror, she checked for stray eyeliner, splashed water on her face, then put on some cherry chapstick.

Many people had mistaken Taylor for a college student despite being twenty-eight years old. Those days were long over.

Taylor picked up her phone and headed downstairs for the door, cursing about driving in the rain. At the doorknob, she remembered she wasn't even wearing any pants, let alone a bra and panties. *Shit!*

Taylor ran back upstairs and slipped into some pink leggings but ditched the underwear. She sucked her teeth, cursing herself again on her way out the door.

Chapter Two

Running a few minutes behind...

Sometimes, Lonnie's pot shop stayed open late and Taylor crossed her fingers that this was that time. Twenty minutes later, Taylor arrived and parked across the street seeing "Queen", the co-owner and some others waving goodbye as they walked away. She hoped Nikki would still be inside.

"Hey! Hey, wait!" Taylor said running up, her flip-flops smacking the pavement.

"What's up Tee?" Queen said looking back.

"Hey! Is Nikki inside?"

"Yeah, she's locking up. Hurry up before she closes."

"Thanks, Queen."

* * *

Taylor went inside and Nikki was taking the receipts from the register to the back.

Nikki had a blow-out hairdo and eighties' look that anyone in the neighborhood would recognize. Her waxed eyebrows made her look exotic especially at night.

"Well, if it isn't my girl Tee coming in this part of town so late? I'm already closed for the evening."

"Nikki, I got caught up with work. I rushed over here as fast I could in the rain and all. I need some—" Taylor whined.

Nikki chuckled, "And you thought that I would be here to help—"

"Please, I just need some smoke to put me to sleep," Taylor pleaded.

Nikki smiled revealing her gold teeth. "No can do, it's illegal after hours, you know. Cops could be watching the place waiting to shut us down," Nikki explained, stuffing her keys into her pocket, "And it's almost midnight anyway, not this time, Tee."

Taylor stuffed her arms inside the sleeves of her big sweater to shield herself from the night's chill. Meanwhile, Nikki turned off the store's light and led Taylor to the door. Taylor's eyes dipped down to Nikki's hand in her pocket and then crossed over to her other one. There was a brown paper bag tucked under her armpit. *Nikki's gotten something for herself...*

Chapter Three

Lonnie's Pot Shop was closed and Nikki and Taylor were outside the storefront. Nikki stared at Taylor; her cat-like gaze seemed to be waiting for something else to happen.

"Ok, I'm going home. No smoke, no sleep..." Taylor said, trying to convince Nikki to give her some. "You got some for yourself, right?"

Nikki raised her eyebrows, glancing down at the paper bag under her arm. She chuckled. "Yeah, I got some samples of some new shit. Queen told me to try them out before we put them out."

"Oh, I didn't know you did all that," Taylor said, "Won't you come by my place so we can try out one or two? It'll put me to sleep..."

"You really don't stop, do you?"

"No, come on. I'm only fifteen minutes away."

Nikki blushed, sort of embarrassed that Taylor is being so insistent but also flirty. She crossed her arms making her midriff rise a little nearly revealing her bosoms. Taylor noticed, fixed herself as Nikki shook her head.

"You know that this could be considered an illegal cannabis delivery in the state of Georgia, Tee."

"I'm not paying you or anything like that. The shop is closed. You're just coming to hang out with some friends in the privacy of my own home!" Taylor replied.

"Friends, huh?" Nikki asked. "Will there be refreshments?"

"Of course! I have orange juice and—"

"Something soft and sweet to eat after we get finished smoking?" Nikki said revealing all four of her golden incisors. A surge of warmth ran through Taylor as she fidgeted in the cold. Their flirtatious conversation admittedly was turning Taylor on.

"Yes, I think so."

"I'll follow you. My car's parked a block away. I know you're the white sedan, right?"

"Yeah."

Nikki headed towards her vehicle and Taylor bit her lip as she watched her walk away. *Look at her, she's so damn sexy!*

Chapter Four

The drive was the longest fifteen minutes of Taylor's life.

Every few seconds, she looked up to make sure that Nikki's headlights didn't suddenly disappear in the fog but they followed steadily behind her until they arrived at Taylor's townhouse.

Taylor's hands trembled as she punched in the keycode to enter the first floor hallway and she hoped Nikki did not notice.

Once inside, they're greeted in the long corridor by the chill hip hop that was playing and soft glow of the lavender lights in the living room. Taylor took off her shoes and turned to say something to Nikki. Nikki already placed her Nikes on the rack next to Taylor's.

"Don't worry about the front door—it locks on its own, everything is upstairs..." Taylor said as she led Nikki down the dark hall.

"Where's your friends?" Nikki asked.

"They must be all out," Taylor said now leading Nikki upstairs.

The living room was just as Taylor left it. Her laptop was on the floor and to her horror, the webcam and her age-play wig were still laying around.

She rushed over to gather up her things, smiling nervously. Then, she gestured Nikki to the couch, "Let me just put this away in the closet. Have a seat? Make yourself comfortable, I'll be right back!"

Taylor tossed her laptop and webcam aside then headed to the closet which was overflowing with her outfits.

She hung her wig up and before she closed the door, Taylor looked herself over in the mirror. *What are you excited about, Taylor?*

Taylor ran her fingers through her hair attempting to fluff it out a bit further.

It'll be fine, she's just a girl who came by to smoke some bud with you. You get naked and fuck yourself for people every night, this is just another person.

Taylor took a deep breath, then turned her head held high and began heading downstairs to the living room.

* * *

It was a strong scent that hit Taylor first; the sound of a flint lighting, and then the familiar bubbling sound of the bong. Sitting cross legged, Nikki leaned back against the pink sofa with the bong from Taylor's fridge nestled in her lap. As Taylor approached, Nikki exhaled a white cloud of smoke without coughing. It hung in the air between the two and the ambient scene made Taylor feel aroused.

"Oh good, you found it," Taylor said, taking her time to kneel next to Nikki and tuck her legs beneath, "How does it taste?"

"Good, very lemony," Nikki said, handing the bong over, "And I hope you don't mind that I—" Nikki's eyes dropped to the bong in Taylor's lap; its neck was so long looking comfortable as it rested between Taylor's breasts. Nikki then leaned forward to light the bong for Taylor.

"I hope you don't mind that I started without you... I

know it's late and you need to get your beauty sleep," Nikki said.

Taylor inhaled the bong deeper than she normally would causing her to cough over and over. Her eyes watered as she heard Nikki's soft chuckles. Then, she felt Nikki rubbing her back.

"Easy, easy," Nikki said, her gold teeth flashing when she smiled, "Bit off more than you can chew, huh?"

Taylor nodded, her eyes were bloodshot red. Nikki reached for the bong.

"Not funny!" Taylor said brattily, "It's been awhile since I've used that thing."

"I could tell by the frost on it when I looked in your fridge." Nikki gestured to the kitchen. "Besides, you almost never buy any real bud, only that weak oil."

Taylor looked like she might argue but knew Nikki was telling the truth. She couldn't remember the last time she bought real weed.

"You're right. I wanted to get some tonight, but you know? Sista could have hooked me up but didn't?" Taylor responded.

"Mmm—I came through for both of us, didn't I?" Nikki said, in the middle of packing another round.

Taylor watched as Nikki methodically emptied out the ashes in a nearby ashtray. She can't keep her eyes off Nikki.

Once Nikki's done, her lips pressed against the top of the long neck before she inhaled. The chamber bubbled and Taylor is entranced with the ritual of it. She wished that she was the bong being handled so carefully by Nikki.

Chapter Five

Taylor was so occupied with that it took her by surprise when Nikki set the bong down and leaned forward. Nikki's lips grazed against Taylor's. White smoke snaked between them for a beat before Taylor realized this wasn't just a simple kiss. Eyes lidding, Taylor steadily inhaled the smoke between them, tasting not only the citrusy terpenes of the weed but also the mintiness of Nikki's breath.

Taylor was the first to pull away and she didn't cough this time. She blew out a large plume of smoke but managed to hold her own. Nikki watched her, her eyes were heavy from the sensation. In the lavender glow above, Nikki and Taylor were in a haven of euphoria.

Nikki leaned back against the couch, patted her lap and murmured, "C'mere, Tee."

Taylor had no choice but to obey Nikki's soft

command. She closed the space between them, kneeled and then crawled into Nikki's lap. Her breath trembled as she felt the weight of Nikki shift as she got more relaxed beneath her.

Taylor felt warm between Nikki's thighs. Even through her leggings, Taylor felt the hardness of her lower body and the lean fat on her belly when she rested backward. Nikki has the frame of a tennis player; every part of her body was tight but relaxed.

Nikki looked up at Taylor, her fingers caressed Taylor's cheek, tracing lightly over her glossy lips, then down her neck, over her shoulder and lastly her arms. Those same hands rested on her thighs and squeezed the clothed flesh as if to test its firmness. Nikki's hands slid upwards but stop at the edge of Taylor's sweater, making clear they will go no further without permission.

Taylor gasped and laid her hand atop one of Nikki's, guiding it beneath the hem of her sweater until she felt Nikki's fingertips against her skin at the edge of her leggings.

"My name is Taylor..." Taylor whispered as she bit her bottom lip, unsure of why she was saying this to Nikki. She inhaled deeply feeling Nikki's fingers curl around her waist and appling pressure to her back. Taylor leaned down, her hands rested on Nikki's shoulders until their heads were inches apart.

* * *

In the background, Taylor's chill hip-hop playlist transitioned to a more up-tempo song. The sound of Nikki's voice whispering, her lips brushing lightly against Taylor's and the mood made Taylor feel wanted.

"So you want me to call you Taylor?"

Taylor shook her head slowly then murmured, "No, I like it when you call me Tee—"

Cut off mid-sentence, Taylor was met with a kiss from Nikki. Her arms encircled Taylor's waist as Taylor clung to Nikki's shirt desperately trying to keep up with the pace. Nikki's mouth tasted of mint, weed, and something else she couldn't identify.

Seconds later, Nikki flipped them both so that she was on top and Taylor was beneath her. They were tangled in the space between the coffee table and the couch. Taylor's legs were parted so Nikki could fit snugly between them. They continued to kiss, clinging to each other and unwilling to yield even as they run out of air.

* * *

Nikki broke next to look Taylor over, as if she is waiting for something but was unable to say exactly what. Taylor bit her lip excitedly taking Nikki's hand in her own and guiding it downward; encouraging her to explore further.

Nikki soon began squeezing one of Taylor's breasts finding Taylor's bosoms perfect in form. That made Taylor arch her back, squirm, and push her hips against Nikki.

Nikki then lifted Taylor's sweater up slowly, exposing her midriff, then rising mounds of her breasts, and lastly her dark nipples. Nikki leaned over putting one and then the other into her mouth. Somehow. Nikki almost sucked Taylor's entire breast in one suckling.

"God, Nikki..." Taylor gasped; she was wet, heated, and uncomfortable in her leggings.

Each time Nikki's teeth landed on Taylor's nipples or sucked them, Taylor tugged at Nikki's shirt moaning lowly. Never did she think that she would be so hungry for a female's touch. Nikki was so gentle and careful handling her body.

Eyes closed, Nikki nuzzled into Taylor's belly and smiled when Taylor's moans turned to giggles as she kissed along. She smelt the arousal between Taylor's legs but resisted the urge to shove her face between them, telling herself not just yet. "You don't know what I was going to do next, do you?"

"It's whatever..."

* * *

That's all Taylor had to say...

Nikki didn't wait long as she pulled Taylor's leggings

down to reveal her trimmed strip of coarse pubic hair and a luscious meaty pink labia. Nikki moaned, "Oh girl, look at what you got there."

"You like it?"

"Oh, hell yeah! You're all meaty in the right place..."

Nikki widen Taylor's legs, marveling at how soft Taylor's hairs looked.

"Taylor," Nikki whispered, her voice deepening, "I need you to tell me you want me."

Taylor nodded, too afraid her voice would crack. That wasn't enough for Nikki as her fingers went further down to the outside Taylor's pinkish lips.

"I mean it. I want to hear you, girl. If you say nothing, I will leave."

Taylor moaned unable to respond as Nikki rubbed near her core. Her fingers were so close to Taylor's clit turning Taylor on.

"Yes, I want you..." Taylor said.

Chapter Six

Hearing how needy Taylor sounded, Nikki began going to work. Her fingers slipped and dipped between the wet folds of Taylor and then started swirling over Taylor's nub.

"Oh, Nikki...I'm so wet..."

"I know, boo. It feels so good, don't it..." Nikki said while rubbing Taylor's g-spot making her raise her hips to encourage her on.

"Let me hear you say my name," Nikki said purring and encouraging Taylor on. "Say my name or I'm going home..."

The tips of Nikki's fingers swung themselves clockwise around Taylor's clit.

"Nikki...Nikki..."

"I can't hear you..."

"Nikki, please...please...Fuck"! Taylor managed to say between gasps, her eyes fixed on Nikki's grill.

The violet lighting above bathed them as they glinted. "God, do whatever you want," Taylor moaned.

Nikki cocked her head as she asked, "Like what, Tee? Tell me what that *'whatever'* is."

Taylor panted, "I've dreamed of you touching me like this before..."

Taylor reached for Nikki's other hand, putting up to her throat to choke her. Nikki's fingers curved easily around her neck.

"Oh, no you didn't," Nikki mused as her grip tightened around Taylor's neck. Her other hand begin thrusting into Taylor. "I didn't think you were one that wanted it like this..."

Taylor didn't respond, nor did she desire to.

Nikki then pushed Taylor onto her back by her neck and towered over her, her hand clung to the shoulder of Taylor's shirt while the other curled it's way around her own thigh to keep her legs spread. Taylor had gotten so wet that they could hear her pussy smack.

Taylor's walls pulsed rhythmically as Nikki's grasp tightened, she had never been so close to what is sure to be a powerful climax. If Taylor could scream, she would have and if she could yell out, she would do that, too. Then just as Taylor thought she might be over the edge, Nikki's grasp loosened and her fingers came to a halt.

"What the—" Taylor said trembling as Nikki's fingers curled then tenderly stroked her wet passage again. Taylor whimpered in disappointment and aching frustration until Nikki rewarded her again.

"Not too much this time, Tee. Next time, we'll talk about how much you can handle."

The suggestion that there would be a next time made Taylor's body heaved as her pussy clenched down over Nikki's fingers. Chuckling, Nikki withdrew them again and Nikki sucked her teeth while making more mewling sighs.

Those sighs were quickly put to rest the moment Taylor watched Nikki suck those same fingers slathered with her cream. Nikki cleaned them off by licking them one by one. Her gold canines flashed as she got up and went on her knees. Her face rested between Taylor's slim thighs.

"Yes..." Taylor moaned.

"Good things come to those who wait, my love..."

* * *

A thrill ran through Taylor seeing Nikki between her. It was followed by a sharp yet somehow pleasurable pain when Nikki sank her golden fangs into the soft, dark flesh of Taylor's thigh. Nikki's hands kept a tight hold on Taylor's hips, holding her in place. Even as Taylor squirmed under Nikki's bites, kisses, and warm licks right outside of reach of her center, Nikki took her time before giving Taylor what she had been whimpering for.

And when Nikki's tongue finally took a long, languorous lap over Taylor's dripping folds upwards to her clit, Taylor gasped aloud, "Ohhhhhhh!"

Nikki creased her brow, pleased and moaned along with Taylor. She tasted even better than she did on her fingers. Nikki watched Taylor suspensefully as she enjoyed her pussy, sliding her tongue up in long, slow licks of her slick velvet petals again and again. Each one drew a shiver, moan, or roll of Taylor's hips to push her pussy further into Nikki's mouth.

Just when Taylor thinks she's on the brink of begging does Nikki finally obliged her; her mouth enveloped her pussy, sucking and drawing it in as though Taylor were a ripened peach. Taylor cried out happily, her high-pitched voice rising among the ambient tones of her playlist. She reachd down to glide her glossy nails through Nikki's cropped hair and over her scalp. Without thought, she held Nikki's head in both hands, keeping her mouth right where she wanted.

"Oh, yes...oh, yes, boo..." Taylor squealed.

The wet sound of Nikki's greedy lips joined the harmony of Taylor's mewls amongst the binaural tones humming in the background. Her fingers sank into Taylor's flesh hard enough to possibly leave bruises but when she tried to draw it back, Taylor whimpers, "No, harder..."

Nikki was more than happy to please her.

She grabbed onto Taylor's hips and holds her down, her glittering eyes darting upwards to watch Taylor squirm in her hands. As she angled her neck just enough to slip her tongue inside, she glid a hand across her skin to squeeze Taylor's breast and pinched her nipple. Taylor groaned and bit her bottom lip as she arched her back, eager to feel Nikki's palms on her body.

Between her thighs, Nikki continued sucking Taylor's clit, lapped at her flushed folds, and dipped her tongue into the core of her good pussy. She paid close attention to what Taylor liked most and did her best to repeat it, pushing her closer and closer to coming.

Nikki was pushing all Taylor's right buttons feeling the tiny pinpricks of nails and hands on her head hold her still. "Right there, right there..." Taylor said. Her moans had risen in an earnest crescendo and Nikki found herself unable to pull away. Nikki's gaze was fixated on watching Taylor raise her hips up and down, bucking the words, *no, no, no. I'm coming baby, Fuckkkkkkk!*

***

Shortly after, Taylor's hips lowered; a thick white paste covered Nikki's mouth. Nikki then slid her tongue along Taylor's lips to gather what was left over.

"Wanted to do that to you for so long..." Nikki said wiping her face.

"Look at what you made me do—" Taylor said, panting on the floor, unable to fully comprehend that her long-time fantasy of being with a girl actually came true. The real thing was so much better. She wondered how Nikki didn't have women crawling over broken glass to get her. Once she caught her breath, she sat up, grinning wider and wider.

Nikki retreated to sit back, her eyes still glittering with lust but patient to see what her host would do or say next.

"That was..." Taylor giggled giddily then shook her head, unable to find the right words for, "I've wanted you to do that for awhile..."

Taylor sat up with an amused grunt, causing her bunched up sweater to fall and cover her breasts. She crawled on her hands and knees toward Nikki, eyes fixed on Nikki's lips still pasted with her wetness in the violet light. Taylor reached over and kissed her wholly and fully. She smelled and tastde her own juices but it only spurred Taylor on to continue further. Nikki groaned enjoying every minute of Taylor's rapture.

* * *

There is a longing to Nikki's stare and Taylor held it, seeming to understand that she has given her silent permission to explore. Blood pounds in Taylor's ears as her hands traced a path over Nikki's shoulders then further down over her small breasts. Her sports bra enhanced Nikki's hard nipples which sent an encouraging thrill through Taylor. "May I return the favor, Nikki? How can I thank you?"

Taylor did not wait for Nikki to answer her, her fingers had already loosened her jeans and begun pulling down her zipper.

"I want you—" Nikki said breathlessly, her voice deepened to a husky tone dripping with *want and need* even in its strained politeness, "Please..."

Taylor's hand slipped easily into Nikki's boxers, brushing over a thicket of pubic hair and quickly finding the heated region. "Look at you all wet and shit..." Taylor said.

"You got me this way..."

Taylor's fingers glid over Nikki's clit and dipped between her folds in a steady rhythm. She kissed Nikki, delighted in every gasp and moan she can draw from her mouth.

"Oh fuck, Taylor..." Nikki moaned while Taylor was fingering her so expertly. Nikki leaned against the couch for support, hard and wet for Taylor from the moment she began following her home from the pot shop. Nikki knows she's only moments away from cumming.

"Yes, fuck yes—!" Nikki moaned against Taylor's lips like a prayer between kisses, hips rolling and rising to meet the increasing pace of Taylor's circling fingers around her clit, "Taylor, oh baby... oh...Fuck...I—"

* * *

Taylor crushed her lips to Nikki's and moaned with her feeling the evidence of just how drenched she made Nikki. Taylor's head dipped back, breaking the kiss to run her tongue up Nikki's neck, to the lobe of her earlobe. Nikki clung to Taylor's sweater as her hips bucked in response.

When Nikki came for Taylor, it was a faint tremor and a long held gasp. "Ayeeeeeee! Oh, oh, oh, mama" Nikki yelled, convulsing and gasping for air.

Taylor pulled her hand out; her fingers were glistening with wetness that was so thick and viscous. She felt proud as she looked at Nikki. Then she sucked her fingers one by one.

"You're so nasty," Nikki said.

"I know boo..."

Chapter Seven

Taylor and Nikki shared a glass of orange juice as they laid side by side on the couch.

"Hey, you know you can stay if you like," Taylor said.

"I think I should go. Your boyfriend might show up seeing me here and all," Nikki said as she rubbed Taylor's arm.

"Don't be like that. I don't have one..."

"Say what?"

"You heard me..."

Both rose and Taylor contemplated telling Nikki about her side hustle as Nikki started zipping and buttoning up her jeans.

"So you're leaving me here all wet and horny..." Taylor asked.

"Boo, I have to get home to feed my cat before it tears up my kitchen."

"Aw, that's so sweet of you."

Taylor walked Nikki to the door and the two exchanged kisses on the way.

* * *

Taylor felt a bit of bittersweetness about their little situation. Happy that it happened, sad that it ended, and worried that it wouldn't happen again.

Once Nikki put her sneakers on, she lingered at the door, watching the Taylor's mood change before her. "Ok, so what's wrong..."

"I don't want you to go—" Taylor eyes rose to meet hers.

"I'll be back. Take my number. You know we won't forget about this night ever—" Nikki said caressing Taylor's face.

"I know..." Taylor said.

"Hmm..." Nikki grabbed Taylor's crotch."You know I want this little Kitty down again..."

"Oh!" Taylor moaned eager to restart and Nikki couldn't help but smile. She leaned down and kissed Taylor's forehead before turning and heading down the walkway to her car.

"Good night, Tee."

"Good night, boo."

Taylor closed the door behind her but watched Nikki until she pulled off and disappeared into the fog.

The End

Rebecca

Chapter One

My name is Rebecca Horowitz, I'm five-foot-six, athletic and blonde. I was drawn to Pam Federman, one of our paralegals, for the same reason as my male colleagues. It was mere lust and I'm not ashamed to admit it. I was a thirty-three-year-old Assistant District Attorney based in Manhattan, New York. I'd been out since high school and it was my boast that the only cock I'd seen was in my brother's collection of dirty magazines. Actually, I'm lying and I'll get to that momentarily.

I was raised in New York City and if you didn't carry a weapon, then you were fair game. I started karate when I was thirteen and by the time I was sixteen; I was taking part in amateur bouts. I wouldn't say I was the best because back then there were very few girls taking up martial arts, that my competitors were somewhat lackluster. The only time I've had to use self-defense is when an officer from a neighboring DA's office crossed the line one night while we were out drinking after a conference. I punched him in the eye and felt sorry for him, so I took him home for the evening and made out with him. Let's just say I crossed that line once.

Who was Pam Federman?

Pam Federman was brought over from Buffalo to Manhattan, catching our male colleagues' eyes the first day she stepped foot through our office doors. The young woman was twenty six years old, five foot seven and had an athletic build. She was good at paying attention to details; some paralegals just talk the talk but Pam walked the walk. You knew when you gave her instructions she was actually paying attention.

Moreover, Pam was well aware of the effect she had on guys around our entire floor. Her sexual preference seemed to indicate she was straight and there was always gossip about how many boyfriends she had in our building.

* * *

I met one supposedly, Jacob Stevens, in the lobby when he came to pick her up for lunch one day. He was a dick in layman's terms, and I see why it appeared to only last one afternoon with Pam. The next day, I asked her about her date, and she seemed dismissive. Nonetheless, I was more concerned about our mayor's demands to clamp down on the recent surge of crime in the city. He was up for re-election and this was one of those cases that proved to be the catalyst that drew me and Pam together.

* * *

There was a case passed onto our office by the sexual assault division and involved an accountant who'd been charged with statutory rape but the case was shaky because the victim had been drinking before the ordeal. On any normal day, it might have gone to a plea bargain or the judge would have thrown out the case, citing circumstantial evidence at best. However, Pam had taken a personal interest in it and got in contact with the hospital the victim had gone to the following morning and here fate turned in our favor because the admitting doctor was a colleague of mine in university. She'd done a blood test to check for other drugs and the test came back positive for Rohypnol. When our office had followed up that line of inquiry, we discovered that the victim had never taken anything stronger than Melatonin. The doctor was surprised when Pam turned up to ask for the report because she thought the police had lost it.

The police called the accused back in for questioning and when confronted with the fresh evidence, he folded like a deck of cards throwing himself at the mercy of the DA's office. Further investigation found that there had been a string of rape allegations from similar women who'd allowed him to buy them a drink. The defendant was sentenced to twenty-five years in prison without possibility of parole. I got a commendation from my superior, which I passed onto Pam that very day.

"So what gave you a hunch to further investigate this one?" I asked.

"Just something wasn't right," she replied, "You know when you get that feeling, right?"

I nodded as I rubbed her shoulder. It felt soft, and maybe I rubbed it longer than usual.

* * *

Therefore, our friendship began from that day on and over the next eight months, Pam became something of a personal legal secretary to me. I mean she had to work with other attorneys as well, but Pam preferred my company because the men tended to either flirt with her or assign her boring jobs. I was the only one who looked past the physical and saw that she really was trying to move up the ladder. You could give her a job and just walk away knowing she'd do it and if she couldn't, there was always a good reason why she hadn't managed to complete it.

When the Feds brought murder and racketeering charges against one of the most notorious crime families of New York, some of our people were brought in to assist the prosecutors. Having fewer staff around meant we had to double up and thus Pam was moved up a notch to my level and I became her supervisor.

A few of my male counterparts were jealous. They knew I was a lesbian and how that came out is a story in its own. I'll tell you how quickly the mayor invited the Fraternal Order of Manhattan Police, Manhattan PD and the DA's Office to a private movie screening to see Red Sonja one evening. It was supposed to be couples-only, but I showed up solo. When an officer asked me why, I told him I only showed up to see Brigitte Neilson (I really had a crush on her sexy ass). He ran away with my comment and to this day, the guy in the department nickname me 'Red Sonja'.

I told Pam the story and surprisingly, this was her response: "Yeah, me too," she said, "Not that anyone would ever know."

"I would," I said and when Pam raised her eyebrows, I finally confessed my sexuality. "I go out with women."

Pam looked past me for a few seconds, looking as if she was ready to leave. I opened my mouth to speak then she asked, "What types?"

"Femmes—I mean I've been out with butches but always been attracted to women who were ladylike."

"I see…"

Our conversation then drifted to other matters but when we were about to part for the evening. I knew Pam was bendable because she told me to walk her home. A walk-home was what it was. In other words, good night and see you in the office tomorrow morning.

Chapter Two

A friend of mine thought I was reading too much into it when I told her about Pam the following day over lunch.

"It's more about Pam getting home, okay," she said.

"If you say so, but..." I replied. "Oh, shit! There she is," I stopped seeing Pam was on her way out of the cafeteria. I didn't notice she had lunch already and told my friend that I'll be back in a minute. I caught up with Pam on the stairwell.

"Hey!"

"Hi."

"Good to see you," I said. My voice was cracking.

"Good to see you, too. I'm—"

"Heading out for lunch?" I caught her off mid-sentence.

"No, I've just had lunch."

"Oh," I said, my eyes shifted to her thighs. "Right, okay," I said as Pam leaned against the rails. Her nipples were poking out of her sweater, and I wanted to scream.

"Maybe we can have lunch together sometime," Pam said.

"Sure, see you later," I replied.

"Okay!" Pam said, then raced downstairs.

* * *

I had the feeling Pam wanted to make a move, and it caught me off-guard. I had to dash back to court to oppose a last-minute bail application. Something that took longer than normal due to a fire alarm going off just before I was about to enter the courtroom. Geez, I can't catch a break!

* * *

By the time I got back to the office, Pam was just about to leave for today.

"You got any plans for this evening?" I said, watching her gather her things.

"Yeah, I have a date, tonight."

"Oh, okay!" I was stumped. "With who?"

"Michael."

"Michael Bernstein?"

"Yeah!"

"Wow! You've never talked about him before," I teased.

"I've been seeing him for the last few weeks, I don't know where it's going."

"He's sort of a—" I said, but mid-sentence, but Pam left the office leaving me hanging.

"Okay—" I sighed.

* * *

I honestly thought that this was going nowhere, Pam might come across as curious at best. I spent the night at home with a Dominos Pizza and six-pack of Coronas watching Disobedience on Hulu because I also had a big crush on Rachel Weisz.

Chapter Three

Pam was a few minutes late the next morning and apologized, which made me suspect that she and Michael both hit home runs. That illusion was shattered when I stepped out of a toilet cubicle to find Pam brushing her hair while her eyes were watery.

"I've had it with men," Pam sighed, "What is it with them that they think buying you dinner entitles them to sex?"

"It's part of their DNA, I guess," I started washing my hands.

"Maybe I'll change sides then," Pam sprayed perfume on her wrists.

"Oh," I stared at her in the mirror, "Okay."

"What're you doing for lunch, Rebecca?"

"Huh?" I turned the tap off, "I—have to put in an

appearance at courthouse, so I don't think I'll have time today."

"Well, how about I meet you there?"

I hesitated before saying yes because I didn't want to seem too eager. Pam grinned as she tucked in her blouse further. "I know you'll be hungry..." she continued.

"Yeah, this felony case is driving me nuts," I said as I was fixing my blazer.

"So, I take that as a yes? By the way, I'm going to Starbucks. What would you like?" Pam said.

"Anything with caffeine."

"Cream—sugar?"

"No, just black," I took my wallet out, "Here, seeing as you're doin' the walkin', I'll do the treatin'. Can you get me a muffin, too? Thanks."

"Got you!"

Pam left leaving me to contemplate this sudden shift in attitude. We weren't the only ones in the bathroom, two of the cubicle doors were closed and while Pam hadn't come out, dropping that comment in a place where women might overhear it could be like blasting it over the loudspeaker. Just as I stepped out of the bathroom, Jane came out of a cubicle which was something of a relief because she wasn't one to gossip.

* * *

My appearance that day was to submit an indictment for a man arrested for embezzlement and because he was over the threshold of the state's limit. We also applied to have his passport seized. Pam helped us prepare the briefs beforehand. Once the lunch recess was given by the judge, I met with Pam at Au Bon Pain.

"The defendant's wife paid the bond but he has to report every other day to his local precinct, let's hope he don't skip town," I said as we waited for our food.

"You think he will?" Pam asked.

"I doubt it. His wife seems to have got him by the balls. I thought she was going to frog march him out of the courthouse. Even the judge was trying not to laugh," I said as they served our food.

"You look so smart in that suit," Pam said, looking me up and down.

"I do?" I looked down at myself. I'd gone for the pinstripe trouser suit look that day with a white blouse, "Thanks."

* * *

I learned a lot about Pam that lunchtime. She was one of four girls in a religious family, her parents were avid churchgoers but only her youngest sibling was still involved.

"Mary's still in high school," she told me, "She enjoys

the church's youth group and this year she'll be a junior counselor at the summer camp."

"So what turned you off religion?" I asked.

"I started hanging out with a different crowd at college," Pam said sipping her Pepsi, "When you get exposed to a different way of thinking, you either make your walls higher or open the gates and venture off. I chose the latter because it was lonely inside my own little castle. When I told mom that one of my friends was lesbo, she warned me to stay away because in her words, the lady was infectious."

"Yeah, been there, done that, I was straight until I was fifteen and then some gay girl sneezed on me and I've been gay ever since," I chuckled.

"You've got a cute smile," Pam nudged me, "Just don't sneeze on me for God's sake. My mom has the prayer circle working overtime to keep me from succumbing to the Devil."

"God, we could be sisters!"

Chapter Four

Our lunch date was over soon enough, but on the way back to the office, Pam and I detoured to Best Buy. She said she was thinking about buying some Beats. Thus, I found myself crammed into a booth with a small window set into the door and a pair of headphones on trying them out, Pam had a test pair on and here's where it got erotic.

The presence of the window prevented us from kissing but it didn't stop her from walking her fingers up and down my leg. It was such a turn on because people were walking past the booth or looking straight at us, totally unaware of what Pam was doing. After a second song, she slid her finger behind the placket of my fly. Then she pulled the headphones off.

"What're you doing tonight, Becca?"

"Apart from work—" I looked at my watch, "I've got catching up to do with some—"

Pam cut me off mid-sentence, "We'll see about that," she hung the headphones up, "I'm buying these and a few other things. I'll see you back at the office."

Pam smacked me on the butt, and I knew it was on from there.

* * *

Pam was as good as her word. I had a mountain of work waiting for me on my desk when I get back. We finished just after six and as I prepared to leave, she seemed anxious.

"Something wrong?" I asked.

"This doesn't mean we?"

"Fuck?" I smirked. "It's on my agenda but first I need to eat. If we fuck afterwards then so be it but if not, I'm not complaining."

"Now that's something I've never heard before. This is interesting," Pam said, reaching under her blouse, "So, if we had dinner and I decided to go home, we'd still be friends?"

"Of course," I pulled the clasp from my hair and shook my hair loose, "Is there any other way?"

"This could either be the best thing I've ever done or

the worst," Pam replied as she fluffed her hair out, "But this doesn't mean I'm coming out. It's bad enough that I listen to Janelle Monáe. If I told Mom, I slept with a woman she'd have a fit."

"It's not about coming out," I said, "Some women know what they want from quite early on but others later in life."

"I'm not saying I've felt like this before," Pam frowned, "Maybe I'm just pushing back against my latest shenanigans with these stupid men."

"I understand," I grabbed my purse, "Look at it this way. You don't have to worry about getting pregnant and no one knows except you and your girl." I opened the office door for her. "And what's even better, you could make out at work and no one would dare fire you."

Pam giggled. "I should remember that."

"Seriously," I continued as we headed to the elevator, "I get how you feel. Girl, I was raised Jewish and we're not even supposed to use any form of birth control. I used to listen to the rabbis at school talking about sex and the right way to do it and wonder who the hell died and made them sex educators."

My words appeared to set the conversation over a meal of pepperoni pizza and red wine forty-five minutes later at my condo.

* * *

"So, what're you looking for in a partner?" I asked.

"Respect," Pam replied, "I want to be an attorney but it seems that all the men I meet seem to think that once we get married, I'll give up my career and become this perfect little housewife. It's why I moved to Manhattan, I thought that maybe men here were different. You meet some okay guys here but I seem to have a target on my back. I keep attracting these paternalistic types who want to put me under a glass dome and keep me there."

"Well, at least I have one with a door," I chuckled, "What am I saying?" I slapped my forehead, feeling tipsy.

"Now that's an excellent question." Pam swiveled to face me, "What are you saying, girl?"

"I might have to plead the fifth on that one, your honor," I took another sip, "It just slips out when I've had a couple of drinks."

"So what happens when I get you started on the next round; maybe a little whiskey?"

"My legs open," I said chuckling, "I had my first taste of heaven's milk when I was thirteen."

"I gotta go pee," Pam leaned forward putting her hand on my leg, "Don't fall asleep on me."

I mused as she went to the toilet but by the time she came back, I had to pee too. Now, I'd have time to ponder my next move or let's just say a few moves ahead. I've always had this habit of thinking ahead. It was something I've picked up from playing chess with my dad. I studied my reflection in the mirror. Damn, she looks so good in there.

Maybe Pam was thinking along the same lines as I stepped back into the living room, She was fiddling with her Rolex while staring at the television. Normally I would have been watching Queer Eye, but I'd turned it down so we could listen to some music.

"I really should get going, it's late..." Pam said glancing at the clock.

"Maybe," I came and sat next to her, "It's been a helluva day!"

"I had a great time today," Pam touched my leg.

"Me too," I put my hand on top of hers.

Pam then cocked her hair back to squint at the light from the ceiling. One of the first things I did when I moved in was buy that shade at the thrift store a few miles away. Unfortunately, it was now showing its age.

"You need to buy a new shade. That light is killing me," Pam murmured.

"Yeah, let me turn it off." I reached over and turned the ceiling light off. "I've been meaning to change it for a while."

Pam giggled. "Okay—so be honest with me now that we're not at work."

"What about?" I asked.

"Did you actually pay for that ugly shade or was it already here when you moved in?"

"I got it from the thrift store."

"Somebody isn't telling me the whole story," Pam squeezed my leg."

"What? I did—okay, it's a shitty shade, I admit." I chuckled.,"I keep meaning to buy a new one but then some case comes up and I just forget. To be honest, one of my exes did buy another one but when we broke up, the shade was part of the settlement."

"You're kidding," Pam's eyes widened, "So along with your heart, she also left you with that old shade, what a bitch!"

"No, she's good. It was more of me than her," I replied, "I came home after work one day and found a note on the kitchen table saying she was breaking up with me and then a list of things she said that she had taken with her."

"What a bitch!" Pam squeezed my leg again, "I would have gone after her."

"To be frank, I was just glad to see Amy's back, she started out as a one-night-stand but then never moved out and seven months down the road, I was getting tired of coming home to moldy cheese and spoiled milk in the fridge."

"That's what I hate about some bitches," Pam said, "There should have been an asskicking waiting for her every time you came home."

"That girl's long gone," I said.

"Well, I have a crazy story, too."

"Ok, tell me..."

"One of my girlfriends had this hidden camera in her boyfriend's room one night for a dare. She got him (the captain of the football team) to confess that he'd had a crush on his mother. She told him if he told the truth, she'd let him have his way with her for that one night."

"Nasty," I said, "And did he do it?"

"Yeah," her eyes shifted, "He was crying when the video came out. Somebody reposted it when my girl posted it on Snapchat between us. We laughed so hard we cried, too. Amy was always twisted. If you told her something couldn't be done, she'd take it as a challenge."

"So what happened to Amy after that? Did her boyfriend beat her ass because I would have?"

"No, he didn't beat her. She left campus and moved to Canada," Pam hooked her elbow over the top of the couch, "Now Amy was one chick I would have slept with, if she'd been interested."

"You don't say?" I adjusted my position, "What made her so?"

"I guess it was the way she expressed herself," Pam responded. "Amy was the hottest cheerleader in school. She was sexy as heck and I would have—"

"So, what if Amy had done this?" My finger moved up to the front of Pam's blouse landing on her top bottom.

Pam didn't budge as I reached the top button, I

expected her to pull back but she locked her hand around my wrist and came forward until we were inches from each other's mouths.

"Your move, counselor," she panted.

"I know."

Chapter Five

My lips brushed across Pam's and seconds later, I undid her second button and was down to her third. She moaned, but still didn't pull back. We stared into each other's eyes, pausing for a few moments, before kissing again.

"I don't know about this," Pam sighed, catching me off guard.

"Don't worry, I do," I panted as Pam moaned in my mouth.

The next step confirmed how Pam was really feeling when she pulled her skirt up and got on top of me.

I reached up and grasped onto her buttocks. Her cheeks were so soft. My fingernails teased her delicate nerves all the while we kept making out. Then, I took a chance and unzipped her skirt from behind and that broke Pam's spell. She stopped kissing me.

"I'm going too fast?" I said, while I was rubbing her derrière.

Pam bit her lip, looking embarrassed.

"No, you're not but—"

"But what?"

"I feel so dirty making out here in your living room. The blinds are open even if we're on the 43rd floor."

"No one can see us from up here except—" I whispered as I breathed in her ear.

"A perv?" Pam said, causing us to chuckle.

"Then off to the bedroom?" I signaled.

"Is that where you fuck all of your girls?"

"Maybe—maybe not?"

"I'm feeling so appreciated right now, Becca," Pam moaned. "You're here at the right time."

"I know..."

I leaned forward and Pam went backwards, I caught her before she could fall and pulled her up. She wrapped her arms around me and kissed me as we skirted around the table and made our way across the floor to the bedroom door. When we got there, Pam stopped and put her hands on my chest.

"I'm not making promises, Becca?"

"Tonight isn't about promises, follow me," I unbuckled her belt and opened the door.

* * *

We stepped inside, and I led Pam to the bed. Her skirt's button popped loose as we reached the bed's end and I pushed her onto it. She plopped startled at my strength. I then turned on the lamp and kicked my shoes off.

"Do you want this?" I showed her one of my dildos.

"Dildo," Pam's eyes widened, "I've never used one before."

"Then let me introduce you to Big Henry." I pulled out Big Henry, my medium-sized one that has seen a lot of use over the years and handed it to her. I recently retired him when I discovered he had a little crack in him, but I knew he was still up to doing the job.

"That's big," Pam held it up.

"Oh, there's bigger," I said undoing my trousers. "Not that I've had a cock inside me lately."

"You haven't?"

"Nope," I pulled my trousers over my hips and they slid all the way down, "Just call me a virgin when it comes to getting dick."

"And I'm a virgin when it comes to this," Pam's eyes raised as I took a few steps forward. My body was so ripe for her.

"Ah, so, we're both virgins," I knelt on the bed, "This should be interesting."

Pam edged backwards as I started pulling her skirt down. She bit her lip as I kept going downward and when it reached her knees. Pam spread her legs and brought Big Henry to her vagina. Then she started moving Big Henry back and forth across her lips. "Wow! This doesn't feel bad at all..."

"Hmm... You look like a putty cat," I murmured.

Pam giggled as she started tickling her perineum. That elicited a low groan from her and I kept going. letting my tongue slick over her lips all the way to her clit and back down again. "Oh, oh! That feels so good!, Becca. Right there..."

* * *

My licks went on for some time whilst Pam continued rubbing Big Henry between her lips. I took over and slid Big Henry inside her. Pam let out a yelp, "Ayeeeeee!" as the tip pierced her. I rested it there for little while as I gave her another tongue bath then put Big Henry in a little deeper. "Fuck, Becca. I'm so yours..." she moaned, and I enjoyed every second.

I slid Big Henry in deeper as I kept up my remorseless tongue bath, I let Big Henry come all the way out not long after only to repeat the process again, this time going in just a tad bit deeper. "Aye, it feels so good... Don't stop!"

Pam fondled her breasts and moved with me. Her moans became more frantic until she snatched Big Henry from me and started entering herself with short sharp plunges. Pam came yelling, "Fuccccckkk!" Her screams almost deafened me.

"Hey, what about you?" Pam asked, reclining back on my bed as she caught her breath.

"That was step one. It's a long night ahead, sweetheart, so lay back and enjoy," I said, rubbing her tits.

Chapter Six

A lot has happened since that night. Pam and I were together for a few months before breaking up after six. She told me that her parents would kill her if they found out. She felt guilty being in a homosexual relationship. Our second time around, I think it was better because Pam finally rid herself of her demons and so-called saints. She confessed she would never desire men again.

We moved to Philadelphia and got married not long after the law granted homosexual couples the ability to marry. We adopted two lovely kids and now we're one big happy family.

The End

Amber

Prologue

The long, magnificently shaped length of Amber Johansson's thigh gleamed like liquid gold in the warm sunshine that angled across the modern-sleek decorated office. Her short purple skirt did little to conceal her long sexy legs. Even the secretary who watched her from behind the plexiglass felt obliged to admire the perfection of the visitor's figure. Despite the constant stream of well-dressed men and women that passed through the doors of 'Cherry on the Top', Amber stood out the most. Her ravishing beauty was one of the reasons why she was waiting outside the office of Thomas Nigel, the owner.

Looking around, Amber smiled, wondering what the other tenants in this office building would have said had they realised that this place was in the business of supplying call girls to London's rich and famous bad boys and girls.

Amber thought back while she waited how she came to work for Cherry on the Top...

Amber Johansson was born and raised in Stockholm, Sweden to a lower-middle-class family. She had just been about to graduate with a degree in Economics when a combination of dirty politics and the Juggemaffian Mafia had ruined her parents, both of whom were found dead in their bedroom, the result of a suicide. Amber had had her doubts as to the real cause of her parents' deaths but was canny enough to keep her mouth shut. Dropping out of university, Amber had found herself on the job market in a country flooded with willing workers and far too few jobs. She soon realized that in order to have any kind of future, she would have to make her way to the West.

For the next few months, Amber made a living by modeling for many amateur photographers who were all over Western Europe. Despite numerous offers, she refused to act in porn films or model for any sleazy magazines and websites. At every modeling session, Amber did her best to make friends and took the opportunity to ask questions. Finally, she decided to set her sights on going to the UK and, through the help of one of her modelling colleagues, she found the right connection. Using a selection of photos from her best modelling shoots, Amber put together a portfolio and emailed over hundreds of potential modelling agencies in Europe and abroad. Thomas Nigel, owner of Cherry on the Top, contacted Amber a week later, inviting her to attend an interview with one of his 'talent scouts' in Stockholm.

* * *

Amber met the recruiter at a high-end restaurant in downtown Stockholm and they talked for over an hour. He asked her about her past, ambitions, and affairs in general. He also quizzed her about her sexual habits and tastes, some which were obscene, to be frank. Amber soon realized that she was being screened and did not allow herself to be provoked by the man's crude insinuations. Finally, the recruiter presented her with an offer. In return for a three-year contract, Cherry on the Top would give her a handsome monthly income, buy her plane tickets to London, and take care of all her visa expenses. Upon completion of the contract, Cherry on the Top guaranteed to pursue citizenship for Amber in the UK.

Since she had little to lose, Amber signed the contract. She was now a high-class escort for Cherry on the Top.

During Amber's first week, she attended a grooming course taught by several of Cherry on the Top's senior management. They familiarised her with the latest fashions, hot gossip that was making rounds as well as the names and backgrounds of the wealthy elite. As part of this course, Amber was required to have sex with a man and woman who, between them put her through just about every sexual activity possible. Driven by determination, Amber graduated with flying colours.

* * *

Amber soon settled in, and for the most part, she found it rewarding, even if the clients that she entertained were sometimes *dicks* for lack of better words.

It's been Amber's three-month anniversary and she had just moved into her first apartment when she received a call from Mr Nigel's personal secretary to attend a meeting with him the following morning.

Amber spent the night trying to remember any offence that might have gotten her into trouble. She imagined every scenario possible. The thought that Amber might be dismissed and sent home terrified her.

Chapter One

Amber had been sitting outside of Mr Nigel's office for nearly half and hour when another woman came and took a seat next to her. Amber had never seen the woman before, but she fit the profile of an escort. She had black hair and was shorter than Amber, dressed in a tight black leather outfit that showed off her taut toned body. The warm musky smell of leather combined with the woman's perfume washed over Amber, who turned to smile and to nod.

'Nice to meet you,' Amber said extending my hand.

'Nice to meet you, too,' replied the woman.

The woman's arrival seemed to act as a signal and moments later, Mr Nigel's personal secretary looked up from her paperwork and motioned for them to enter Mr Nigel's office.

* * *

Thomas Nigel, the owner of Cherry on the Top, was in front of a couch, smiling. A low table was set out with English tea and biscuits.

'Welcome ladies' said Mr Nigel, holding out his arms as if to embrace them. 'Sit, please,' he said, indicating the armchairs to either side of him. 'Tea'?

Both women nodded as Mr Nigel cleared his throat.

'I am so glad to meet the two of you today. It is not often that I get to talk to the troops, as it were,' said Nigel, sounding like a caricature of the typical old school boss. 'I suppose that I should start by introducing you to each other. Amber, this is Ava, Ava, Amber'.

The two women nodded to each other, and at the same time took an assessment of each others' assets and appearance.

Mr Nigel set down his tea cup and continued. 'Cherry on the Top has been approached by a very prominent client, who has made a rather unusual request. Because of its priority and importance, I have personally picked two of our best new employees for this job'. Mr Nigel nodded, glancing at each woman in turn. 'Ava, if you accept and perform to the client's satisfaction, you will be paid ten times your usual rate. Amber, your reward will, I suspect be even more welcome. If you do well, Cherry on the Top will waive the remainder of your contract's term as well as arrange for your citizenship documents'.

Amber felt her heart leap upon hearing Nigel's words however, the bland smile on the face of Mr Nigel brought her back to reality. Nigel had not stated what was required of them yet.

'I will not do anything criminal, Mr Nigel. Also no egg donor stuff or selling drugs' said Amber. Out of the corner of her eye, she saw Ava raise her eyebrows.

Mr Nigel was shocked at Amber's suspicions of him. 'No, no, nothing like that at all, young woman,' he said, shaking his head. 'Let me explain before you rant further... Our new client is Barbara Adair, ex-wife of Rupert Adair who was the CEO of one of the largest defence contractors in the European Union.

'Mrs Adair came to hear about us from a good friend and has expressed an interest in our services'. Nigel's manner changed as he started talking, looking more like the high-class pimp that he really was. 'She has requested that we supply two young ladies for a light S&M session...'

Ava nodded. When Nigel looked at her, she shrugged and said, 'Why not'?

Amber hesitated before saying, 'Oh, what the heck, Mr Nigel? Why was I picked for this one'? Amber asked unimpressed about being selected.

'Actually, Mrs. Adair picked you from our pinup

catalogue,' replied Nigel, his eyes narrowing at Amber's lack of enthusiasm.

Amber suddenly realised that she did not have a choice, she just nodded and smiled while changing her tune. 'Oh, okay! I was just worried that I would not suit this woman's tastes,' Amber said, 'I'd be pleased to be of service'.

'Good,' said Mr Nigel, rubbing his hands together like a shopkeeper who had just clinched a big sale. 'Remember, Mrs Adair is paying top dollar, so anything short of serious injury in on the menu,' Mr Nigel said, raising an eyebrow.

The women nodded and Amber could not think of an additional response that truly resembled being enthused.

'The two of you, be ready to go to Mrs Adair's home at 2 p.m. tomorrow...' Mr Nigel stopped short of saying *Amber, you may go*.

Seconds later, Amber realised that she had been dismissed and rose to leave. Nigel waved at her. Ava had not made a move to leave yet, so Amber hesitated.

'Go ahead, Mrs Johansson. I have something else to talk over with Ava'.

***

Amber walked out of the building, feeling cheap and seconded to Ava. Her mind was filled with conflicting thoughts and emotions. She had never been beaten even by her parents. As Amber sat in the back of the taxi on the way home, she gingerly pinched herself on the thigh trying to imagine herself with Mrs. Adair while her body was in pain.

Once she got home, Amber sat on the edge of her bed, staring at herself in the mirror. *The prize was worth the price* she told herself until she dozed off.

Chapter Two

Amber spent the next morning at the hairdressers and working on her body, shaving and trimming her pubic hair and lotioning her body. After a light lunch, she was picked up. Ava was already inside the limousine wearing a black wool skirt which had a slit up the side almost up to her hip, a dark brown turtle-neck sweater with matching boots and a creamy leather jacket. Amber was surprised to see a phone clipped to Ava's waistband. It was against the number-one rule of Cherry on the Top - *no cellphones*.

Ava noticed Amber's facial expression and said, 'Orders from the boss. He wants to make sure that everything is to Mrs Adair's satisfaction,' she said, tapping the phone with her fingernail. 'Don't worry. I'll switch it off when we get inside'.

The car pulled up in front of the main gate. The security must have been given the car details because the gate swung open before the driver had a chance to reach for the intercom. Once outside Mrs Adair's, the driver opened the doors for the ladies. They stepped out gracefully as the butler stood by waiting.

'Mrs Adair is waiting for you in the living room'. The butler said as they approached. 'Come this way please'.

* * *

'Your visitors are here, Madam'. He stepped aside and ushered Amber and Ava into the room.

'Close the door, Edward. We are not to be interrupted for any reason unless I call for you,' said Mrs Adair, rising from her chair. She waited for the door to close and for Edward to walk away before she spoke. 'Welcome. I have been looking forward to seeing you. You must be Amber, and you, Ava'. Mrs Adair nodded at each of them, making no move to shake hands. The women waited for Mrs Adair to indicate how she wished to proceed.

'Sit down and let's chat for a moment. And oh, please call me, Barbara'. Mrs Adair waited a few seconds before continuing. 'Let me give you a little background so that you will understand what I want from you, ladies'. She paused gathering her thoughts. 'I married my husband for his money, and he knew that. We got along very well and made a good team...'

Barbara grinned. 'You must be wondering what the point of this rather prosaic tale is all about. Well, I am a good-looking woman and intelligent enough to make him a suitable partner. However, he chose me for another reason. You see, in the bedroom, he was a sadist. He enjoyed hurting his women'.

Amber and Ava glanced at each other. *'What the fuck'!* Their faces expressed.

Seeing this, Mrs Adair laughed, her melodious voice confusing the girls. 'No dears, I was not the poor victim. Shortly after my husband and I had met, he told me all about his tastes in *"entertainment'*. I was the one who gave up my conservative ways in exchange for a very good life. Unlike battered women—God bless their souls, I was always affectionate in public as well as being available for fun and games whenever Mr Adair was in the mood. When we found out that he had a brain tumour, we, of course, were in shock. At the end, my husband said that I was the only person in the world that he had screwed that had not tried to screw him in return. To my surprise, he left me everything and not a cent for anyone else. Mrs Adair nibbled on her lip lost in thought momentarily.

Suddenly, her mood brightened. 'In fact,' she said, 'All the legalities were settled yesterday. Tomorrow, I'll have full control of all my husband's bank accounts, patent rights and shareholdings'. She giggled. 'My late husband did so love his toys. He set this house of ours up with the most sophisticated of security systems. At least, he knew I needed to be taken care of like many other things in life he did'.

Barbara Adair stood up and twirled. Her dress flared like a cloud caught in a gust of wind and Amber and Ava viewed her hot mature body. 'You might say that you two are little gifts to myself to celebrate the occasion. Actually, my husband's best friend of mine gave me the idea. When I said that I bore my husband no ill will for his treatment of me, I meant it. However, I find deep down, in a dark corner of my mind, I've always felt that other women were making fun of me and I hated it'. She stared at Ava and Amber. 'I tell myself that millions of women would have done the same thing if given the chance, but I need to see it for myself'. Pointing at Ava, Mrs Adair asked, 'Do you understand what I want'?

Ava grinned and shrugged. 'Yes, I believe so. I'm here to show you a good time, Barbara. If you want to tan my butt or slap me around, I'm all yours'.

Mrs Adair winked at Ava then turned to Amber, 'And how about you'?

Amber considered Ava's attitude and thought about what Barbara had said. She took a step forward and took hold of Barbara's hand with both of hers. Bringing it up to her lips, she kissed the tips of her fingers and then pressed Barbara's hand to the side of her face. Slowly, Amber ran it down her jaw and curve of her neck until it rested on the upper curve of her breast. 'Barbara, I do not know how sadists play, but I do know about my own body. I know what feels good and what hurts. Usually people want me to tell them what feels good and where I like them to touch me. But I will show you all the soft, tender, sensitive places that will make me moan, cry and scream. I will spread and open myself, so that you can reach all the secret, wet, delicate spots with your fingers, hands, teeth and whips. I will kiss and lick you while you do what you want with me. I'm all yours to play with, Madame'.

Barbara looked into Amber's eyes and saw strength, determination and humour. She squeezed Amber's breast and nodded. Then, she lowered her arm and went back to her seat. 'Let me see you naked. Both of you. Take off all of your clothes, then stand in front of me'.

Amber and Ava finally felt relieved to be undressing gracefully in front of Mrs Adair. It was a sign of approval; one of the first things an escort learned on the job.

Chapter Three

Ava set the phone down on the table and pulled off her clothes tossing them aside as if glad to be rid of them, her tanned slim body radiated. She walked with a swaying confidence away from her garments, stopping an arm's length away from Barbara. She then touched the front of Barbara; all the way from the top of her breasts, across her nipples to her stomach.

Amber was less of an exhibitionist. She neatly folded her clothes as she removed them, setting them aside on a chair, baring her body without the showmanship of her colleague. She kept her high heels on, as she joined Ava in front of Barbara.

Barbara leaned forward and reached out to touch the girls' thighs. The feel of their warm flesh made her eyes light up. Her tongue flicked across her lips as she allowed all her vengeful fantasies of past humiliations fill her mind. She slid her fingers up their inner thighs, stopping just before she touched their buttocks.

'Let's play a little game,' said Barbara. Reaching under the coffee table next to her chair, she pulled out a riding crop made from black leather. 'I want both of you to play with yourselves. Stand right where you are and spread your legs a little'. She waited as the two girls obeyed, shuffling their feet apart until they stood like soldiers. 'Now use the fingers of one hand to spread yourselves and show me your clits'.

In tandem, Ava and Amber reached down and spread their outer labias, bringing their pink inner labias into view. Pulling upwards slightly, they drew the hood of skin back and away from their clits.

'Very good, ladies,' said Barbara. 'Now I want you two to play with your clits. Don't touch anywhere else. Just those sexy clits of yours'.

Amber lifted her finger to her mouth to wet it.

Barbara shook her head and said, 'No, don't do that. Don't use any lubrication'. She waved the riding crop in front of the girls' hips. 'This is a challenge. The winner gets her bottom caned with this crop,' Barbara said, 'And the loser gets caned on her pussy'.

Amber and Ava started to gingerly stroke their clits, wincing.

'By the way, ladies...' said Barbara. 'I have not decided whether the one who cums first or the one who climaxes second shall be the winner. Perhaps I will toss a coin. But let me warn you, I will punish anyone who tries to fake an orgasm or does not want to cum for me. Do you hear me'?

Ava groaned *yes* and closed her eyes in concentration, rubbing her finger in circles around her clit. Amber used a different technique, keeping her fingertip on one spot just above her clit and moving her finger in small side-to-side movements. Both found it difficult to stimulate themselves to reach a climax without being able to touch the rest of their bodies. In addition, the pressure of being competitive made it all the more difficult. Despite Barbara's warning, both had no choice but to try and climax first in hopes of avoiding the more severe punishment.

* * *

Amber's legs and buttocks quivered with the strain of standing with her feet apart as she strained towards an orgasm. She longed to be able to caress her breasts and nipples, finding that the need to concentrate only on her clit was actually making it more difficult for her to cum. Her dry finger was starting to make her clit sore and Amber knew that she was in a race not only with Ava but with her ownself. She had to bring herself to a climax before her touch became too irritating for her to be able to come. She concentrated on the bud that thrust out between her fingers, letting her feelings of shame and excitement over displaying herself to Barbara in this obscene manner add to her stimulation. Her clit tingled as Barbara watched her crotch closely. Each movement of Amber's finger sent a throbbing sensation that rippled through her body to her clit. The sweet aching soreness of her clit, blended pleasure and pain.

* * *

Barbara turned her attention to Ava, who was flickering her clit aggressively, ignoring the discomfort. She braced her hips, pushing against her hand as she panted. Her eyes were shut as she drove herself to an orgasm.

Barbara watched fascinated as both girls masturbated, their moans and groans escalated as they neared their climaxes nearly at the same time. Mrs Adair watched Ava's eyes glance towards Amber, then she grinned seeing the muscles of Ava's belly ripple and clench in small staccato motions signalling her orgasm. Ava's hips bucked and ground as if she were thrusting against her lover and her thighs clamped shut, trapping her hand between them.

Seconds later, Amber cried out wordlessly as she finally drove herself over the top. She staggered as the intense sensation made her knees go weak, but she maintained her widespread stance and continued playing with her clit, drawing out her climax into a series of mini-orgasms.

Barbara saw Amber's clit throbbing and twitching as she came and came. The opening of Amber's vagina glistened with creamy fluids that threatened to drip onto her carpet.

Amber maintained her position and spread her pussy wide, so that Barbara could see the stiffly erect petals of her inner labia and the deep red flush of her flesh. She mentally cringed at the thought of being whipped on her pussy.

* * *

Mrs Adair clapped, 'Bravo ladies. That was an excellent performance'. She then took out a coin, flipped it in the air. 'And the winner is; the one who came last'!

Ava grunted while Amber sighed.

Waving the crop, Barbara then said,' All right, let's give out the prizes. Amber, you first. Keep your legs the way they are and bend over for six'.

Amber bent over and put her hands on her knees, eyeing the nasty-looking crop. The crop and its wielder moved out of view behind her and she clenched her teeth. Despite her concentration, the crop's swishing through the air barely had time to register in her mind before she felt it strike across her buttocks. The hot, stinging pain filled both cheeks of her tautly-stretched buttocks as Amber rocked forward from the impact.

'Count them please,' said Barbara.

'One'! gasped Amber.

Swish...crack!

'Ow! Two'!

The third stroke caught Amber right at the junction where her thighs met her buttocks, and the tip of the crop drew a tiny drop of blood, painting a red bruise.

Amber yelped, her fingers clamping down on her knees as she struggled with her instincts to jump up and rub her buttocks.

'Three'!

The fourth and fifth strokes followed in quick succession, scribing two more straight crimson-coloured lines across Amber's bum.

Barbara took careful aim and brought the crop down hard for the sixth and final stroke. This time, the crop struck only one cheek and the tip sank deep into the crevice between them, right at Amber's asshole.

Amber jumped up, reach around with to shield her ass. However, she still shouted out 'Six'! and thus ended her ordeal.

* * *

Barbara touched Amber's burning skin, enjoying the

heat and the feel of the stiff crimson edged ridges that she had put there. Amber leaned against Barbara.

'Did it hurt a lot'? asked Barbara.

Amber shook her head, caressing Barbara's arm. 'It doesn't matter,' she replied. 'As long as you are happy'. Amber smiled tearfully. 'You can hit me some more if you like'.

Barbara kissed Amber on the cheek and smiled. 'That's enough for now, little one. Ava is waiting to play with me'. She hugged Amber and the feel and scent of the beautiful brunette's body in her arms refilled her senses. Amber felt the crotch of her panties getting stickier.

* * *

Meanwhile, Ava had her arms folded as she watched Amber's caning, but her smirk quickly disappeared when both women looked towards her. She pointed with her nose at the crop in Barbara's hand and said, 'My turn now, I guess. So how do you want me? Sticking my butt up like Amber won't work if you are going to hit my pussy'.

'Why don't you suggest something, dear'? replied Barbara, tapping the crop in her hand.

Ava looked around the room. 'How about I lie on my side on the couch. I can lift my leg up and apart so that you get a good shot'. She suited her words with action, demonstrating the pose. With her forearm hooked behind her knee, Ava was able to hold on to her leg with both arms, which would help her to keep her legs spread wide even when Barbara hit her.

'That looks good' said Barbara, tapping Ava' pussy lightly with her crop. Ava's pose opened up the crevice of her privates to such an extent that Barbara could see right into her vaginal passage. The sight of her gaping pussy gave Barbara another idea and she turned to Amber who was still rubbing her buttocks.

'Amber, I want you to do something for me while I entertain Ava'.

Amber nodded.

Barbara pointed with her crop. 'See that shiny black and silver vibrator over there? I want you to put it in your pussy and turn it on. Turn the dial slowly, one click at a time. I want to see how far you get by the time I'm finished with your colleague'.

Amber said 'Okay'. When she picked up the vibrator, it was heavier than she expected. The shiny strips that ran down its barrel were metallic and cool to touch. Amber then placed the tip at the opening of her vagina and gently rotated from side to side, working it inside her. It slipped easily in because of how wet she was from masturbating.

She glanced over at Barbara, who was playing with Ava's pussy lips, lightly slapping at the moist petals with the tip of the crop. Amber then looked down between her legs remembering Barbara's instructions to turn the dial one click at a time. She turned the dial, feeling it click under her fingers. To her surprise, there was no discernible hum or motion. Then she felt a tiny tickling sensation that ran all along her vagina, making her inner muscles squeeze on the object. She gasped softly, realising that the 'vibrator' did not contain a motor at all. The weight that she had felt was due to a large battery. The metal strips on it's outside were not merely decorations but were actually electrical contacts. She tried turning the dial in the other direction in order to switch the tickling current off, but it would not move. The switch was designed to turn only in one direction unless hidden catch was released. Cautiously, Amber turned the dial another stop. The current grew in strength, and was now strong enough to feel like she was suffering from pins and needles. Her eyes widened. There were a total of ten stops on the dial and if the second was any indication, the higher levels would generate a severe shock and might even burn her flesh at the points of contact. Barbara had wanted to see how far up the dial that Amber would go! She was determined not to disappoint her, so she turned the dial again. The stinging sensation got more powerful, now feeling like ant bites that went on and on. Amber was sweating as the painful throbbing began to spread through her lower body. Just then, a sharp *'smack'* came from the other side of the room. Looking up, Amber saw Ava's body jerk as the crop hit her pussy. Barbara said, 'I shall leave the number of strokes to you. Just tell me when you have had enough'.

* * *

Amber turned the dial again. The sharp pain made her head jolt back while she clenched into the muscles of her bruised buttocks. This level was as far as she could bear if she was to stand here and wait for Mrs Adair to finish whipping Ava.

Meanwhile, Barbara brought the crop down again with a sharp flick, hitting Ava across both of her plump outer labia. Several red marks now decorated Ava's mound and her inner labia had started to swell, too. Ava had drawn her knee right up to her face and hugged her thigh to her chest. She watched as Barbara swung the crop back for another stroke. The whip flashed down in a blurred grey arc before striking Ava's flesh. This time, Barbara had aimed the crop so that only the tip struck her victim, landing right at the upper juncture of Ava's labia and expending its full force on and around her clit.

Ava shouted, her leg kicking at the couch as if to push her Mrs Adair away.

Barbara knelt down beside Ava and asked 'How many of these do you think you could take'?

Ava shook her head, still panting. 'I don't know. That really hurts'.

Barbara said, 'Give me a number, young lady. If it is reasonable and you manage to hold still for them, I will stop beating you'.

Ava blinked as she tried to decide on the minimum number of blows that Barbara was likely to accept and that she would be able to bear. 'Five'? she said hopefully.

'It's a deal'. said Barbara. 'Now open wide, young child'.

The crop cut through the air and hit Ava's clit again. She moaned and writhed. It felt as if her clit had been cut by a knife. The second stroke fell like an explosion in her groin. The skin around her clit was turning a deep sullen red and the bud had swollen to almost double its normal size. Despite her determination, Ava lowered her leg in an instinctive move to shield her genitalia.

'That's naughty,' chided Barbara. 'Let's see that lovely little clit of yours,' she said, waving her hand.

Ava sobbed jerking her thigh upwards, exposing her pussy again. When Barbara swung the crop and tapped her clit with a practice swing, a drop of urine escaped from her urethra as she shrank backward from the blow.

Deciding that Ava deserved a reward for her fortitude, Barbara placed the tip of the crop at the opening of Ava's vagina. 'Hold this for me, dear' she said as she pushed the shaft of the whip into Ava's pussy.

The crop looked like an anorexic penis as Barbara turned towards Amber. Reaching out, she cupped her breasts, toying with her nipples with her thumbs. 'What setting are you at, my dear'?

'Four,' said Amber. 'It really hurts...' she added, bowing her head 'I'm getting wet'.

Barbara kissed her forehead. Then she put her index finger on Amber's clit. Pressing on the moist bud, Barbara felt a tiny tingle on her finger that was the residue from the stinging current that was cracking in Amber's cunt. Gripping the clit, she pressed her lips to Amber's ear. 'I want to hurt you just a little bit more. May I'?

Amber took a deep breath and braced herself. 'You may,' she whispered back. Barbara's lips pressed against hers and they kissed. At the same time, Barbara pinched her clit firmly, her fingernails biting into Amber's flesh. She felt the girl's hot breath as she gasped as well as the her moans that vibrated in her mouth as she continued to squeeze and twist Amber's bud. Just then, the computer on the nearby table gave a beep. 'Oops, sorry. I have to stop for a moment. Money calls,' said Barbara.

As she walked past Ava, she snatched the crop from her fleshy sheath and gave the girl a smack on her clit. 'I don't want you getting bored,' she said laughing.

Chapter Four

Barbara bent down to look at the screen, seeing the message that she had been waiting for the last few days. The cursor on the screen highlighted the words *Enter your desired password, which should not be shorter than 15 digits and may contain letters and numbers.* She typed in her password and hit *Enter*. The screen went blank momentarily and then flashed the words, *Congratulations. Your password has been accepted.*

Barbara whirled around and clapped her hands. 'At last! All of it is mines'! Skipping back to Amber, she gave the girl a kiss on the cheek. In her joy, she did not notice Ava getting up from the couch and staring in the direction of the computer. Suddenly, the green notification button on Ava's smartphone on the table lit up. Ava got up and kicked aside the crop that Barbara had dropped on the floor, and picked up her jacket.

Barbara was reaching for Amber's nipples when she heard Ava clear her throat loudly. Then she saw Amber's eyes widened. Swivelling around, Barbara gasped at the sight of Ava holding a small black gun.

'Do you like it'? asked Ava, waving her gun. 'It's a girl's gun and fits just great in a jacket pocket without making an unsightly bulge. It's so light to carry'. Ava tapped the gun with her hand. 'I'm sorry that I can't cock the hammer back with a click like they do in the movies but I already have chambered a round. I'm sure that you ladies know what to do,' she said, pointing at the ceiling.

Barbara and Amber raised their hands.

'What the fuck is going on here, Ava'? Amber said.

'Shut the fuck up'! Ava screamed. 'I'm in charge, now'.

'Young lady, if you don't stop...'

'I said *Shut the fuck up,* didn't I'? Ava said again. 'Since neither of you are karate experts, I'll risk taking a moment to explain. See that phone over there? It's actually a device which was given to me by your dear late husband's best friend'. Ava grinned at Barbara. 'Yes, the same one who gave you the idea of hiring us for your fun and games. Since he was the one who put in your home's security system, it sure wasn't a problem discovering how to break in,' Ava said laughing while pressed her hand to her pussy. She hissed from the pain.

'You would not dare use that gun in here,' shouted Barbara.

'Are you thinking about your faithful butler'? asked Ava. 'When your husband left everything to you, his faithfulness took a sudden nose-dive. He will earn his share by ensuring that none of the other staff are around to witness what happens'. Ava laughed as Barbara's shoulders sagged. 'In a moment, I will press the '*send*' button on that phone over there and my partners will get your password and begin transferring all... I mean our money to its new home'.

'Why all this rigmarole'? yelled Amber. 'You could have just pointed that thing at Barbara and asked her to give you the password without all this freakin' pain...'

Barbara nodded.

'Sorry,' said Ava shaking her head. 'I knew all about the alarm that would trigger if the wrong password is entered. Had to be cautious, you know. A little pain won't hurt forever'.

'So what happens now'? asked Amber.

'No, my dear. Please just take what you want and let me go,' Mrs Adair said.

Ava shook her head. 'There will be a terrible scandal. Rich perverted lady hires prostitutes for kinky S&M session. The hooker objects to the rough treatment and pulls out a gun. They struggle and the rich lady gets shot. However, because of the small calibre of the pistol, the wounded rich lady manages to snatch the gun and shoot the hooker in the heart before bleeding to death herself'. Ava said as she gingerly touched her swollen clit again. 'I think that you will have the unusual honour of being shot in the pussy,' she snarled. 'Spread you legs apart, Barbara. I want to get a good clean shot'.

'Christ, no! What if I refuse'? Barbara's face began turning pale.

Ava shrugged. 'I have lots of bullets. I don't mind shooting you in the knees and shoulders first. Now let's get on with this. I don't have all day'.

Barbara slowly shuffled her feet apart.

'Ava, I can't be part of this. Just let me go. I don't care what you do after that'?

'Oh, I can't, sweetheart. I'm sorry, but I'll take care of you,' Ava winked.

'What the fuck is that supposed to mean'? Amber asked.

'I said what I said...' Ava looked at Mrs Adair. 'Mrs Adair, let's proceed'.

'Could I ask a favour before you shoot me'? said Mrs Adair, apparently resigned to her fate.

'What'?

'Could you at least let me take that out of Amber's pussy before it happens'? replied Barbara, pointing at the dildo.

Ava laughed. 'It would make the perfect news story to have her found with that thing still in it, but...okay, go take it out'.

Barbara knew that this was her cue. A single chance at living. Now or never.

Amber rolled the dial to six before Barbara took it out. Then, Barbara tossed it at Ava, saying 'Here, you go. Catch'.

Ava swatted at the flying object when her fingers touched the wet metal contacts. A spark arced out sending a searing shock through her hand and up her arm. She screamed from the blast, *fuck*! It stunned her for a second, which was sufficient time for Amber to dive forward and grab the gun.

Ava's finger jerked and a slug whizzed past Amber's ear. Although the bullet did no damage, the blast so close to her head that it had her dazed. Mrs Adair tried wresting the gun away from Ava and for a several seconds, the two girls struggled. Ava managed to break free and pointed the gun at Amber forgetting momentarily about Barbara. She was about to press the trigger up when there was a sharp '*crack*'. She fell to the floor, resulting from Barbara hitting her with the computer.

'My husband always said that computers could be bad for your health' gasped Barbara, dropping its remaining parts on the floor. The two looked down at Ava who was unconscious but still breathing.

'I'm so sorry, Mrs Adair. I had no idea'!

'It'll be okay…' she responded.

Chapter Five

The police had come and gone, taking Ava and the traitorous butler with them. After giving their statements, the police left the two women and ushered away by Barbara's new lawyers.

Amber slumped on the couch, sipping at a glass of brandy.

'What's the matter'? asked Barbara, sitting next to her.

'Well, with my boss in jail and his company shut down, I'm out of a job. Without a sponsor, I will have to leave the UK and go back to Sweden' sighed Amber.

Barbara looked over the beautiful blond for a moment and then she smiled. 'My ex-lawyer may have been a crook, but he did have a good idea. I was enjoying myself up to the point where Ava decided to change the script'.

'You mean you would take me in'? asked Amber.

'I still have a lot of frustrations to work out and you

were much more fun than Ava. We'd make a good couple, don't you think? Now, I have a whole lot of money and time on my hands' said Barbara.

Amber sat still for a moment, still feeling the pain from earlier. Then she smiled and started looking around the room. 'Where'd that crop go'?

'Then I take that to mean *yes*'? asked Barbara.

'If I get what I want, I'm yours,' said Amber, now waving the crop.

'Please don't hurt me, young lady'.

'Oh, I will tonight. It's my turn'.

www.ingramcontent.com/pod-product-compliance
Lightning Source LLC
LaVergne TN
LVHW012023060526
838201LV00061B/4435